REPURPOSED
Life

Lyn Morris

Repurposed Life
Lyn Morris
Heartalk Press

Published by Heartalk Press, Manchester MO

Editor: Kay Uhles
Book Design: DavisCreative.com

Publisher's Cataloging-In-Publication Data

(Prepared by The Donohue Group, Inc.)

Names: Morris, Lyn (Lyn A.), 1958- author.
Title: Repurposed life / Lyn Morris.
Description: Manchester, MO : Heartalk Press, [2020]
Identifiers: ISBN 9781734943405 | ISBN 9781734943412 (ebook)
Subjects: LCSH: Carpenters--Fiction. | Wood--Fiction. | Anthropomorphism--Fiction. | Life change events--Fiction. | Self-actualization (Psychology)--Fiction. | LCGFT: Romance fiction. | Paranormal fiction. | BISAC: FICTION / Romance / General.
Classification: LCC PS3613.O77385 R47 2020 (print) | LCC PS3613.O77385 (ebook) | DDC 813/.6--dc23

2020

*Dedicated to loved ones who no longer bless
us with their physical presence but continue to
influence our lives each and every day.
A very special note of gratitude to my mother,
the source of my inspiration and motivation,
Ethel Buntin.*

It is said when one door closes another one opens. To some this is merely an expression, said in order to give one encouragement during a difficult time.

I didn't buy into this type of half-hearted, sympathetic nonsense until my life became a perfect example. Once a broken shell of a man, with only his dog, Digger, as confidant and companion, to finding love and the desire to look forward to life's next adventure.

Previously, I only viewed my lifetime of carpentry as a way of provided a living. Through events with Digger, the discovery of reclaimed wood and unexpected Spiritual help I was able to move beyond the obvious and open doors to dimensions beyond the tangible. Most of all it restored my heart to love once again.

I now believe and trust in the process of life and the continued discovery and rediscovery of one's life's purpose.

Doors closing and doors opening with lessons learned along the way.

Chapter 1

"Okay! Okay! Digger, you got me," I mumbled as he attempted to get me up and out of bed.

Our usual game had begun as I covered my head and dug in deeper into the covers in an attempt to prolong the inevitable. Digger would use everything at his disposal to find fault in my temporary blanket cocoon. Hardly able to contain his excitement, he bounded on and off the bed and finally stopped long enough to fill my face with big wet doggie kisses. There was no going back to sleep after this unusual but effective alarm clock and that was how every day began since Digger was a pup.

We ambled through the kitchen to the backdoor. I let Digger out and shook my head as I surveyed the yard full of holes, giving it an appearance of green Swiss cheese. Digger has earned his name, and the surrounding area reflected his greatest passion.

The kitchen was a bit messy for some people's standards, and dishes from last night were stacked in the sink. The walls could have used a fresh coat of paint and the appliances reflected their age. The continuous refrigerator hum was comforting in the otherwise quiet house.

The house had been handed down from one generation to the next and sat high enough on the last fifty acres of the original family farm to see the lake in the valley beyond the hayfields. Through the years there had been construction and modernization done to the old farmhouse. Each generation of carpenters made unique changes to the historic home, and it served as a monument to their talents and exceptional craftsmanship. I had given the matter some consideration about what my contribution would be to this living memorial but temporarily came up empty.

I mostly kept to myself after Judy passed and didn't leave the property except for an occasional trip into town on Sunday for church and supplies. Neighbors and friends would stop by once in a while with casseroles and polite conversation but these visits became fewer and fewer as conversations became awkward and forced. No one really knows exactly what to say when these events happen to people. I appreciated their generosity and kindness, but their presence would only remind me more and more of Judy and the deepest hurt possible.

I was ten when I first met Judy while riding my bike on the gravel road that ran alongside of our cornfield. A few yards in front of me was a girl with long dark hair, skipping and giggling as a large yellow butterfly circled around her head. The two seemed to be dancing together and I was captivated by their performance. At one point she stopped and extended her hand for the butterfly to rest upon. She then appeared to carry on a conversation with the winged insect. Eventually, she gestured a small wave goodbye with her free hand and the butterfly took one last lap around her head before it departed. She then bent down and picked up two rocks and placed one in each hand. She slung the rock from her left hand skyward, aimed and hurled the other rock from her right, successfully having both rocks meet in midair. I was impressed and said, a little louder than expected, "Wow, that was cool!" With a slight turn of her head she looked in my direction and smiled. I suspected she knew I had been watching her all along. I waved and pedaled my bike closer to find out more about this interesting girl. From then on Judy and I were like two peas in a pod. Everyone knew we would end up married and no one was surprised when we made the announcement. We married in our early twenties and had just celebrated our five-year anniversary the month before she passed. I towered over Judy in height but she stole the show with her personality. I am a fairly tall man at six feet seven with enough muscle strength to tackle the largest of projects. I inherited my dad's build and was blessed with my mom's blonde hair and blue eyes.

After our marriage, I continued in the family carpentry business. There wasn't anything made from wood I wouldn't make or give it a go. Judy was a great seamstress and also did upholstery work which suited her well.

Judy stood slightly lower than my chest and wore her long black hair in a ponytail almost every day. Her eyes were as dark as black olives, and her eyelashes were so long and thick people would ask her if they were false. Her Houma Indian heritage gave Judy her beautiful complexion and was instrumental in Judy's knowledge of making high quality, intricate and delicate attire. Judy never wore a store-bought garment her entire life and was often asked where she bought this or that garment she was wearing. She would proudly announce she had made it; she would then flash them a smile and give them her business card. Judy got a lot of clients that way, and I was envious of her salesmanship abilities.

We made a great pair both in life and furniture-building and enjoyed a reputation for high-quality work. Judy finished each of our projects with flawless upholstery detail. From fine attire to seat cushions, Judy's talent with material and a sharp needle was obvious in all she touched. We both enjoyed changing raw material into something beautiful and were each other's biggest admirers and critics. Having Judy in my life as far back as I could remember made finding my way without her difficult.

Judy passed two years ago in a car accident during a heavy downpour. We both knew the old car's tires were getting worn, but neither of us thought about the dangers of hydroplaning. She was just going into town to deliver an altered prom dress, a quick trip she said. When she didn't make it back within a reasonable time, I knew deep in my heart something terrible had happened. The local sheriff made a house call with the news her car had slipped off the road and slammed head-long into a tree causing the life-ending traumatic injuries. Hearing the news, my life crumbled along with my body on the living room floor.

A couple of years earlier, Judy and I adopted a pup from the local farmers market one Saturday afternoon.

A dog was something we both talked about adding to our family, but it wasn't until Judy spotted the "Free to Good Home" sign that it quickly became a reality. We had no idea what breed he was, but Digger proved to be a hound through and through. After Judy's death, Digger was my pal and became my lifeline. We would often mosey on down to the lake together. I would cast a line or two, attempting to fish, and Digger would just be himself. Finally, after using up all of his energy, he would plop down next to me looking for an ear rub, and a few kind words before proceeding to stretch out in the sun for a nap. Knowing he needed me as much as I needed him gave me a reason for living. Most of our conversations were one-sided but somehow Digger knew when I needed him most and would get as close as possible to let me know he was there for me. Digger became my constant companion, and I started taking Digger almost everywhere I went.

One morning I realized it was time to get back to work. I had been down long enough and counted on work to help take my mind off of Judy and pull me out of the depression pit. As my dad would say, "The time has come for you to pick yourself up by the bootstraps and get on with living life."

I had a few pieces of wood stacked in my shed but not enough to make anything large enough to sell at H&E Furniture Store in town. Having done business with them for years, I wanted to take them something equal to the quality furniture-building they had learned to expect from Judy and me. And now, just me. Once again, Digger was there to help me out. He discovered some weather-worn wood while with me on a road trip. With no one in sight at the time, it made perfectly good sense to load the wood into the truck bed and take it home.

Taking great care, I unloaded the wood into the shed one piece at a time. It looked well-worn and many years old, and I wondered what type of wood I would discover hidden beneath the aged surface.

Digger eyed me with a puzzled look on his face when I scolded him to leave the wood alone as I removed the load one piece at a time. "I'm not playing with you now. You just leave it where I put it down, no more running off with it, ya hear?" Along with digging, fetch was his next favorite thing. I never knew what treasure Digger would bring me next. Once at the lake, he proudly dropped a large snapping turtle at my feet and displayed the same puzzled look when I jumped backwards, dancing a jig, yelling, "No, Digger, no!" while trying to avoid the snapping jaws heading my way.

It was getting dark by the time the wood was finally unloaded.

"Digger, time for dinner!" I yelled.

Digger appeared almost instantly at my side, and we walked back to the house. After dinner we were both tuckered out and didn't last long watching TV before nodding off. But before heading off to sleep, I made sure to thank God for the gift of the wood. I was grateful for something to keep me busy and, best of all, the wood didn't cost me a dime.

Chapter 2

I awoke the next day with an enthusiasm I had not felt for a long time. The wood Digger and I found was waiting for me to reveal its hidden character. As soon as I began to sort and stack the wood, a voice flooded into my head. Being a woodworker for many years, ideas and creative thoughts were part of the process. But this wasn't my thought; it was more like a voice that seemed to have been coming from outside of myself. Almost as if someone was whispering in my ear. A different tone was apparent, almost feminine and very demanding. At first it began as a distant whisper but then began to increase in volume, insisting I follow its instructions in each step of the reconditioning. The voice kept repeating the need to have each process finished quickly. Time was apparently critical to its plan.

I had been a carpenter all my life, raised by a carpenter, and had many years of experience, both passed down and learned. I resented this unwelcomed voice dictating each step, insisting on every detail, even down to the grain of sandpaper to use. With a tone of irritation, I said aloud, "I know how to plane, sand, and restore wood!"

Realizing I had just argued with what may be a figment of my imagination, I decided to take a step back and retreated down to the lake to clear my head. "Come on, Digger, I need some air." Walking the path, I questioned my sanity: Was this a part of grieving? Was I losing my mind? I was unsuccessful in my attempts to make logical sense out of it and sure didn't want to ask anyone for advice, fearing what they would think of me. So after a while, Digger and I returned back to the shop. Confused but also curious, I reluctantly began the process of reworking the wood as the voice instructed. I felt like a puppet being pulled by invisible strings to do the voice's bidding. The wood was stripped, sanded, planed, and neatly stacked on the workbench. When finished, the wood's once-weathered exterior revealed a beautiful rich walnut underneath. Half-heartedly, I gave the voice some credit for the success of the restoration.

Satisfied with the day's progress, Digger and I headed for the house. I was mentally and physically worn out and could use some peace and quiet.

The next day I opened the double doors of the shop and inhaled the familiar smell of freshly cut wood. I loved that smell. It always took me back to the days I spent watching my dad working and teaching me the trade in this very shop. The interior is a handyman's dream. Various hand tools, passed down through generations, were displayed on every wall. A mix of various machinery, power tools, and a vacuum system were strategically placed around the room. An over-sized workbench occupied the center, reflecting the shop's carefully thought out versatility and functionality.

"The wood is to be made into a unique and special mirror." The voice started as soon as I stepped into the shop. I shook my head from side to side and belliger-ently decided to make the wood into something of my choosing and something I knew would sell at H&E in town. Totally ignoring the voice's demands, I began measurements for an entryway table. I ignored the warning from the voice. I would soon regret my actions. Being set in my determination, I reached for the first piece of wood from the workbench to begin the table. That started an avalanche of wood to tumble down and entrap my feet. When I was finally able to lift one foot out, I took a step forward only to be hit right between the eyes with a board. Dazed and off balance, I stepped back only to be hit square in the back of the head by another. Down on my knees accepting defeat.

"Okay, you win! I get the point!" I shouted at the voice.

I turned and saw Digger standing in the doorway with his head cocked to one side. "I'm not talking to you, Digger; it's this dad-gum voice in my head." Satisfied he was not at fault, he circled and laid down with his eyes fixed on my every move. His way of saying "Okay, but I'm not leaving you alone."

"Thanks, buddy," I called to him, and Digger's tail wagged in acknowledgement.

I stepped into the shop's bathroom and reviewed the damages in the mirror. Satisfied it wasn't worth a trip to the hospital, I began cleaning up the mess, first my face and then the shop. When the wood was restacked, my head pounded like a sledge hammer from all of the bending over and lifting. Feeling frustrated, I took a seat on a nearby stool and decided to present my case to the voice.

"How is this project you're insisting I make ever going to be done without plans? A design, measurements, something. Give me something to go off of." I pleaded aloud.

Once again, Digger sat up. "Still not talking to you," I said. With a sigh, Digger dropped to the floor turning his face away from me. I suspected he was a bit aggravated at my outbursts.

The voice responded to get some paper and something to write with. Sitting in front of the paper, the design started rapidly spilling out; my hands were no longer under my complete control. Within minutes the dimensions and plans were illustrated. Impressed with what I was looking at, I couldn't help marvel at the unique detail and design. The project was to be a full-length mirror with mirrored wings on each side that could easily be adjusted for viewing. The wings were designed to fold over and fit into the curvature of the main mirror's frame when not in use and still leave enough mirrored surface to see one's entire reflection. A sturdy easel-like back frame allowed the mirror to stand on the floor and support the entire piece. Special hinges would be used for the wings to be adjusted. I had to admit the design would be a challenge to build, and I was excited to get started. Using the measurements according to the plans, it became evident it was going to take every last piece of the restored walnut.

"No room for error," I said aloud to no one.

Ever since the wood-bashing experience, I was more than happy to let the voice take the lead. The special hinges and custom mirrors were ordered from suppliers and I got to work on the frame. It took many days and nights of cutting, sanding, assembling, and applying layers of varnish. Finally, the mirror frames were ready for the finishing touches. Fortunately, the special-ordered mirrors came in the following day and fit perfectly into the openings of the frames. Carefully, I attached the special hinges for the wings and stepped back to admire the piece. Everything had worked out as planned, and it turned out the voice and I worked pretty well together.

The voice stressed the importance of getting the mirrored piece into town and on display early, before H&E Furniture opened this coming Saturday.

"Was hoping to get a little more rest," I argued back to the voice, but knew it was useless.

At least I had two days all to myself, one of which was occupied with cleaning up the shop. Another of Dad's tips: a clean shop was essential for success.

Chapter 3

Saturday morning the mirrored piece was loaded into the truck with great care. Layered foam was stretched out in the truck bed and more was used with moving blankets to wrap and secure the main mirror. I carefully removed the wings and wrapped them separately. I double-checked my tool box, made sure I had everything necessary to reassemble the mirrors, and closed the tailgate. Digger had a sincere look of disappointment when I gave him the news, he wouldn't be going with me this time. Knowing he had access to the house through a doggie door, I assured him he would be fine until I returned from town.

"Be a good boy and no parties," I told him rubbing his ears before getting in the truck and heading into town.

Libertyville is located halfway between Shreveport and Alexandria, Louisiana. The town square looked like a million town squares across the country. The courthouse was located in the center, surrounded by various shops and the famous Ruby's Diner. Walking into

Ruby's was like walking into a time-warped museum. Ruby's favorite color was red and the diner reflected her personality. Shiny chrome tables and chairs sat on a traditional black-and-white tile floor. Table and counter tops, chair and stools, and even the ceiling fans were all ruby red. People loved the diner and often more local business was done in Ruby's than the courthouse.

Ruby's specialized in homemade breakfast, mile-high pies, and the best coffee around. Every day Ruby's offered a blue-plate special that would leave you satisfied and draw you back for more. Ruby's reasonably priced menu was mostly due to Fred's Butcher Shop and Smoked Meats located next door. Fred and Ruby had an on-and-off again relationship for years. They were pretty independent people, and their heated arguments could be heard throughout the square; but when they combined talents, it was a mouthwatering experience served at Ruby's. The trip into town gave me the opportunity to enjoy a hot breakfast at Ruby's, and my mouth watered in anticipation.

H&E Furniture was located on the corner directly across the square from Ruby's. Among the other shops around the square was Ray's Hardware. Ray was the go-to man for any plumbing, electrical, woodworking, or home-repair advice and supplies. If you couldn't do the job on your own, Ray would volunteer to help, even if it meant closing his store, which Ray was known to do, especially if it was an emergency. His service and concern for his customers was why Ray's Hardware had stayed in business despite increased competition in the larger cities with the big box stores. Alongside Ray's, there's the 5&10 Store that carried everything from boxed candy to sewing needs. Judy would make a trip into town every week or so to see their latest fabrics. Next was Gallery A, the local artists' hangout. The second floor above the gallery was converted into a large studio where local artists were free to make and then sell their creations in the gallery below. Beside Gallery A was Magnolia's Flowers and Gifts, a great place for the softer side, offering fresh flowers, handcrafted soaps, and a dress shop. Rounding out the main shops is the 2&4 Beauty Shop and Pet Grooming. The 2&4 Beauty Shop and Pet Grooming was a fancy salon where you and your pampered pet could get beautified at the same time, nails and all. Digger and I would never step into such a place, but it was a big hit with the ladies for miles around. No telling how much gossip was exchanged within those walls. More shops, the church, library, and other businesses were down the side streets.

The town was an easy place to walk and take in a slower pace of life. The sidewalk was lined with trees and park benches, making it comfortable even during the hottest days of the year. The Ladies Flower Club maintained the front and back of the courthouse's expansive park-like grounds. Every season they would be busy planting and arranging flowers along the sidewalks, walking paths, and pagoda. The pagoda sat in the back of the courthouse grounds and became a popular place for small weddings and celebrations. Grateful for the extra revenue and the ladies' hard work, the mayor commissioned a large fountain and dedicated it in their honor. The fountain was located directly across from the pagoda, and the setting was often used as a backdrop for wedding and graduation pictures.

Tourists, escaping the winter weather, resorting in the nearby lake area, or traveling to and from the colleges and universities, often stopped for a bite at Ruby's Diner and to take a step back in time with Libertyville's unique shops and southern charm.

I arrived in town earlier than expected and counted on the extra time to unload, reassemble, and get the mirror in position on the sales floor before H&E's doors opened. H&E Furniture has been a fixture on the courthouse block for over thirty years. When I was a kid, I often rode in the truck with my dad when he brought his work to a furniture store on the very same corner. The name and ownership have since changed over the years. Today, H&E offers the finest locally handcrafted wood furniture and accessories available in these parts. Furniture sold at H&E had a reputation of being passed down from one generation to the next. Each piece was warranted by the original woodcrafter for repairs and/or restoration for life. H&E's commitment to quality and exceptional warranties explained the longevity and devoted following of their customers. I have sold many pieces to them over the years, but not anything like this. I looked forward to their reaction to the mirror. As I drove around the square, I waved and nodded to folks, some known and some not, but in town you always waved. You never knew who you'd meet later down the road.

I backed the truck up to the dock and heard Hil giving directions. Always concerned and cautious about his dock, Hil would direct all delivery trucks himself.

"Just a little more. Okay, you're good. Go ahead and cut it," he shouted over the engine.

I jumped out of the truck and shook Hil's hand. "Morning, Hil."

"Why so early this morning? You called and said you were bringing something for us but didn't think you'd being here this early."

"Well," I said, "I'm counting on getting this set up and in your store before it opens."

"What's your hurry?" Hil asked.

"I have been thinking about Ruby's biscuits and gravy all morning," I replied.

"Yes, sir, I love those Ruby's biscuits and gravy too, but Ethel won't let me get them very often, too much cholesterol, she says." He chuckled.

Hil held the doors while I removed the mirrors from the truck and loaded them onto a dolly. Pushing the dolly through the back of the warehouse, it struck me how clean and organized everything was. The concrete floors were polished to a shine, and racks and pallets sat neatly arranged along the walls allowing for plenty of room to maneuver.

"Ethel!" Hil bellowed, "Come to the back." Knowing Ethel well enough, I knew this was not a good idea. One thing I knew for certain was Ethel didn't like being yelled at for any reason.

I sprinted into the office and greeted Ethel before things took a turn for the worse.

"Hello, beautiful," I said with a big smile and outstretched arms. I saw her frown turn into a big smile when I rounded the corner and stepped into the office.

"Hi, Jim, so glad to see you! Come give me a hug." Ethel has a reputation in the town for hugging everyone. No one was a stranger to Hil and Ethel, and everyone was greeted as if they had been friends for years.

"We've missed you. Hil told me you were bringing us a real gem today."

"Yes, there is a little assembly for me to do first, but then I'll come get you when it's all set for your approval. It's not like anything I've ever made before."

I was very proud of the results, even though I really couldn't take all of the credit, but I wasn't going to open that can of worms. Hil deliberated on whether to set it up in the bedroom area or with the wall mirrors displayed closer to the front of the store. He finally decided that by the wall mirrors made the most sense because there was enough floor space to spread the mirror's wings.

"Okay, Mrs. Ethel, you can come take a look now," I said standing in the office doorway. Ethel made her way through the store looking around for something new on the floor.

"Well," she said a bit frustrated, "where is it?'"

"Over there by the mirrors," Hil answered.

"Another mirror? We don't have enough mirrors?"

"Not like this one," Hil said.

When Ethel got close enough, she spotted the mirror in its full display of glory.

"Oh my! It's beautiful," she exclaimed. "The walnut wood is beautiful and I love the design and functionality. I'm tempted to consider keeping it for myself."

Hil quickly jumped in. "Don't you think you have enough stuff already? We have mirrors all over the house to see yourself in. Why do you want this one?"

Ethel turned to Hil and explained how the wings of the mirror could be adjusted to allow a person to view their appearance from all sides. "With a small turn in front and adjusting the wings, one could even get a view from the back," she said while demonstrating with the mirror's wings.

"Ethel, if there is anything a person our age doesn't need to see, it's their backside that close in a mirror!" Hil said and looked around at us. Ethel and I laughed while nodding in agreement.

I excused myself and quickly went outside to move my truck away from the dock. Then headed back into the office where Ethel was finishing up the paperwork.

As I entered, she offered some advice. "You know the price you are asking for that mirror is a steal for the quality and beauty of that walnut wood, not to mention your time and talent invested."

"Yes," I agreed, "but something tells me there is a special someone this mirror was made for and the price has to be just right. I'm here to tell you it will be gone before the day's end."

"Well, that will suit me just fine, that way she won't be hounding me to buy it and haul it home." Hil said as he appeared in the office doorway.

"Oh, go on and open the store, Hil," Ethel said waving her hand dismissively.

With that, I took my cue to leave, said goodbye to all, and headed towards Ruby's.

As I crossed the street, an attractive young couple walked towards me heading straight to H&E. We exchanged greetings before we each continued on our paths. With Ruby's within eyesight, my mouth began to water with anticipation.

Chapter 4

"Ding, Ding," the chime above the door rang, announcing the couple's arrival at H&E. Hil had just turned the "Open" sign around and greeted them with his usual smile for the ladies and a firm handshake for the guys. Hil loved to greet the customers, and his friendly and inviting personality came through to everyone.

"Hi, I'm Hil. What brings you in today?"

"Hi. I'm Brian and this is my beautiful wife, Jacquelyn."

"Hi, Hil, please call me Jac," she said while offering a warm smile.

Brian continued, "Today is Jac's birthday and we are interested in purchasing a full-length mirror."

Hil couldn't believe his ears, and it seemed to take a while for Brian's request to register before responding.

"Please, follow me. We just got a beautiful mirror in this morning from a local carpenter, and it may be just what you're looking for," Hil said as he walked the couple through the store to where the mirror was displayed.

Proudly, he demonstrated all of the mirror's qualities and versatility, while stressing the beauty of the walnut wood.

"Not just a finish or veneer, but solid walnut," he explained. It was apparent they were impressed and Hil went in for the sale. "You're the first to see this piece."

"It's perfect! I know it's bigger than we talked about, but I'm sure it will fit in the corner between the bay window and the bath," Jac said looking into Brian's eyes.

"Well, Hil, I guess you better write it up. Jac's made up her mind," Brian said. "Happy birthday, Sweetheart."

Brian had pursued a law degree at the same time Jac was focused on a Doctorate of Veterinary Medicine at LSU in Baton Rouge. An animal rights demonstration and a crowded bus sparked the beginning of their relationship. Originally from Shreveport, they decided after graduation to settle down in a small town somewhere in between the two cities to work and raise a family. They had visited Libertyville many times on the way to and from Shreveport and jumped at the chance when an opportunity was offered to Brian. The resident lawyer in Libertyville was interested in taking on an attorney to assist him and eventually help him move into retirement. Not soon after Brian got the job, their ideal farmhouse came on the market and they quickly moved in. Jac came up with the idea to build her animal clinic across the drive from the house. The property was located just outside the city limits making it possible to service both large and small animals. Their dream was coming together and their lives seemed to be written like a story book.

Brian started noticing a change in Jac's appearance not soon after they moved into the farmhouse. Jac was a beautiful woman, tall and slender; but Brian noticed, since moving into the house, Jac seemed to be getting thinner and thinner as time went on. His rational mind blamed it on her increased activities and workload. Brian then noticed Jac's lack of appetite. Constant questioning and pushing for her to eat only made things worse and Jac's attitude more defensive. So when Jac wanted a mirror for her birthday, Brian was a bit confused.

"Really, are you sure a mirror?"

"Yes, I would like to get a good full-length mirror for the bedroom, made from real wood, not like the cheap plastic one currently in the closet," Jac replied. As it turned out, the mirror at H&E was perfect for Jac's birthday present and Brian was relieved to see her happy.

Jac's veterinarian clinic was only a hop, skip, and a jump from the house. This was especially convenient for deliveries and other housing appointments. Although the bedroom located on the second floor was easily accessed by the large staircase, the weight and mass of the mirror made it cumbersome and difficult to move. Carefully, the H&E delivery men ascended the stairs; and after taking a much-needed moment to catch their breath, Jac directed them to the exact location to set up the mirror. She thanked them and then returned to the clinic, pleased with the new addition to their bedroom. She was excited and could hardly wait for Brian to see how perfectly the mirror fit in the space and reflected light from the bay windows throughout the room.

Brian didn't get a chance to say hello when Jac greeted him at the door and announced the mirror had arrived.

"You have to go upstairs and see how great it looks," she said.

He did as Jac asked and was equally impressed with how it completely changed the lighting in the room. The natural light from the bay windows reflected off the wings and illuminated the darkest corners of the bedroom.

The next day over breakfast, Jac said, "I'm so excited about this weekend's mayoral ball!"

Brian was forced to dress in a suit and tie every day for his clients and court. Jac lived in smocks and jeans. So Brian knew the opportunity for Jac to dress up was fun and exciting. Besides Jac always loved a party.

"Looking forward to being your plus-one and dancing the night away," Jac continued. Shock then flashed across her face.

"What's wrong?" Brian asked, puzzled at this sudden change in her attitude.

"I have to get a dress! There is nothing in my closet that would fit right or be fancy enough for the event."

"Oh, the old 'I have nothing to wear routine,'" Brian teased, but knew she was right. When Brian first met Jac, he thought she looked like a porcelain doll. Her thick auburn hair against her light skin and green eyes made her the most beautiful women he had ever laid eyes on. But the recent excessive loss of weight changed her once-beautiful porcelain-doll appearance into sickly and haggard. Brian noticed she had hardly eaten any of her breakfast even though she had taken a decent portion of food. Brian knew Jac's latest eating habits. She would take longer than necessary to cut up whatever was on her plate and then push it around, only taking one or two bites. It was a game he had seen her play with food way too often, and it appeared to be getting worse.

Jac's day had gone pretty much on schedule, a few regulars and one emergency, but nothing out of the ordinary. Finished for the day, Jac walked to the house and up the stairs to change out of the clinic attire. That's when things started to get interesting and somewhat confusing. As usual, Jac removed her work attire and went into the closet for a change of clothes. Passing the old closet mirror, she caught a glimpse of her naked reflection. Not happy with what she saw, Jac grabbed the loosest and baggiest clothes in her closet.

With clothes in hand, Jac made her way across the room and headed for a quick shower. Jac stopped dead in her tracks and dropped the clothes she was carrying at the sight of her nude reflection in the newly delivered mirror.

"I look like a walking skeleton. What's happened to me?" As if seeing herself for the first time, Jac positioned the wings of the mirror to assess the entire view. Appearing bony and malnourished was not what she had learned to expect from her usual reflection in the closet mirror. Turning her back to the conflicted appearance, she picked up the clothes and proceeded into the bath where a hot shower would somehow make everything better.

After the shower, Jac left the bathroom and gathered up a load of laundry to throw into the wash while waiting for Brian. She purposely ignored the mirrors and concentrated on looking anywhere but into either of them until she could make some sense out of what she had witnessed earlier.

Brian's return home for dinner was perfectly timed, just as Jac pulled the meatloaf out of the oven. Brian smelled the aroma as soon as he opened the door. "Hello there. Boy, something really smells good in here," he shouted down the hall, grateful it wasn't salad again. "What have you got cooking, good looking?" he said as he kissed her while glancing around the kitchen looking for the answer.

"Meatloaf, haven't made it for a long time, and I know it's one of your favorites. With all the trimmings, too!" Jac replied.

"Terrific. Wait, what's up?" Brian asked thinking there was more to the story.

"Nothing, just felt like surprising you tonight. Go on up and change while I make the gravy for the mashed potatoes."

"I'll be back in a flash," Brian shouted as he sprinted up the stairs two at a time.

After dinner they discussed their day as Brian cleaned up the kitchen. They took turns cooking and cleaning up. Jac usually made dinner and Brian made breakfast. Jac decided not to mention the mirror mystery and listened intently to him as he went on about the office events.

Brian was pleased to see Jac's renewed interest in dinner; and he wasn't absolutely certain, but he thought he actually saw her eat a few more bites off her plate than usual.

The next day was a repeat of the day before with the conflicting mirrors. Jac surprised Brian with meatballs and spaghetti. This was totally unexpected as pasta was banned from the house shortly after moving in. Once again, Brian witnessed an increase in Jac's appetite and again nothing was said by either one about the changes taking place.

Each went to bed with questions and thoughts that sooner or later would have to be addressed and brought out into the open. Brian was happy to see Jac doing better and didn't want to spoil it by asking too many questions. Jac was concerned about the differences in her reflection from one mirror to the other and was worried that the new expensive mirror that she just had to have might be from a carnival fun house.

Next morning at breakfast, Jac announced she didn't have any appointments for the day and she was going shopping in the city for a dress.

"Are you going with anyone?" Brian asked a bit concerned.

"Yes, Mom and I are having a girls' day of shopping and then lunch. Would you like to join us?" She teased.

"No, thank you, not my idea of a good time. Don't worry about getting back before dinner, there are plenty of leftovers."

"Okay, I will text you when I'm on my way home," Jac replied.

"Perfect, be safe and give Mrs. Gloria my love," he replied as he kissed her goodbye.

Jac's mom was waiting on the veranda in the swing when she pulled up, just the way Jac always remembered her. The swing was an anniversary present from her dad over twenty years ago. A little aged but still in good shape. It brought back fond memories and her mom would sit in it for hours.

"Hi, Mom!" Jac said as she walked up to the porch. "How are you today?" she asked, kissing her cheek.

"Pretty good, darling, and you?" Gloria replied, but saw for herself how much thinner Jac was since the last time she had seen her. Determined to enjoy the day together, she let the observation go for the time being, but made a mental note to call Brian ASAP!

Gloria was an attractive women, and anyone could see they were mother and daughter. Gloria used a little help from the hair salon to keep the red in her hair, but her sea-green eyes were full of life and her whole face lit up when she smiled. She still had an attractive figure and kept busy with friends and volunteering at church. Shorter in height than Jac, Gloria loved her high heels, which made up their height difference. Jac knew Gloria loved her heels but could only tolerate them for short periods of time.

"Did you remember to bring some comfortable flats?" Jac reminded her.

"Already ahead of you. That's what is in this here tote," Gloria responded, pointing to the bag slung over her shoulder. Arm-in-arm, they walked to Jac's car with the anticipation of a successful dress-hunting day.

Their first stop was Royal's Fine Attire, their usual go-to when looking for formal dresses.

"Look who just came through the door. It's Gloria and Jac as I live and breathe. Hello, you two. How are you?" Margie greeted as she embraced them with the usual welcome hug.

"Haven't seen ya'll since Jac's wedding. What brings ya'll in today?" Margie asked while she took a mental note of how thin Jac had gotten and wasn't too sure she had anything in the shop small enough to fit her.

"I'm looking for a semi-formal dress for the Mayor's Liberty Ball this Saturday. Mom is helping me by making sure the dress is suitable for an up-and-coming lawyer's wife," Jac said with a little laugh while making quotation marks with her hands.

"I remember your taste runs a little on the, well, shall we say, not conservative side," Margie said chuckling. "Jac, it looks to me ya'll have lost some weight, not that you had much to lose. Have you been sick, child?" Margie asked with a serious note of concern in her voice as she assessed Jac's measurements.

"Oh, no, not sick at all, just super busy with the clinic and new house," Jac quickly replied.

"Well, sweetheart, let's take a look at ya and find that special dress," Margie replied, not buying into Jac's explanation. Gloria and Margie exchanged knowing looks of concern.

Margie and Gloria selected various dresses and passed them into the dressing room.

"No! No! No!" Was all they heard coming from behind the door. "They all seem to be too big and I'm swimming in them!"

"Well, sweetheart, that is one of the lowest sizes I carry in the shop. Let me see if we missed anything. Be right back," Margie said motioning for Gloria to follow her out of hearing distance from Jac.

"Gloria, Jac has gotten way too thin. What is going on?"

Gloria nodded her head in agreement as tears welled up in her eyes.

"Brian and I have talked about this, but I had no idea how bad it had gotten. Every conversation with Jac about her weight always ended so badly. Jac had always been so active and they run and bike a lot," Gloria offered.

"Gloria, you should see her without her clothes on. I suggest you have a very serious talk with her," Margie whispered.

"Hey, I'm getting cold in here, are you still bringing more dresses or are we done?" Jac shouted through the door.

"Sorry, sweetheart, your mom is coming with some more now," Margie replied as she loaded up Gloria's arms with dresses in the smallest size she had. Margie wanted Gloria to see what Jac looked like without the baggie pants and oversized top.

Jac couldn't believe what she was seeing in the dressing room mirror. The first set of dresses hung limp from her body like a wet rag. She had always worn a small size, but Jac noticed none of her curves existed anymore and everything hung in a straight line from her shoulders, reminding her of pictures she had seen of starving people.

Jac opened the door for Gloria to get the next round of dresses but didn't like the concerned look on her mom's face. Gloria forced a smile at Jac, but it wasn't easy to see her daughter's body in its current condition. Fear rose in her throat, and she tried hard not to let Jac see the tears that were filling her eyes. Gloria quickly closed the door. Margie opened her arms and offered a hug along with a much-needed tissue.

After a while Jac stepped out of the room in a traditional black tea length dress.

"This one works, but I guess you know it's way too traditional for me. I wanted you to see this one before I show you the one I really like."

"Okay, darling. It's a possibility but you do look a little uncomfortable in that high neckline and all," Gloria responded, grateful for regaining her composure. Jac took one last look in the mirror and headed back to change. Soon reappearing in a deep royal blue dress.

"Girl, you dazzle!" Margie clapped her hands and exclaimed. The see-through material on the arms masked the lack of flesh, and the form-fitted bodice before the skirt flared into multiple pleats gave the appearance of curves where there weren't any.

"So, Mom, do I dazzle or blend in with the crowd and go black?" Gloria knew Jac had already made up her mind and agreed.

"Go blue and dazzle, baby!" Satisfied with their decision, the blue dress was purchased, and they were soon on the way to a celebratory lunch.

"Mom, would you mind if I borrowed your purse with the crystals?" Jac asked on the drive to their favorite restaurant.

"I knew one day you'd find a way to get your hands on that purse. Just bring it back or I'll come hunt you down where you live," Gloria teased.

"Okay, but I just might keep it and make you come get it," Jac teased back and they both laughed.

Jac and Gloria enjoyed their time together at lunch, updating each other on current events in their lives. Gloria carefully watched Jac eat while trying not to be too obvious. She made mental notes and planned to share her observations with Brian.

"I love my heels, but I'm sure glad to put these flats on," Gloria said as she slipped off the heels when they got back into the car.

"I wondered how long you would keep them on. I don't know how you do it," Jac said.

"Would you want to come in for a while?" Gloria asked as they pulled into the drive.

"Thanks, Mom, but I better be getting back home."

"Okay, I'll be back. Going in to get the purse," Gloria said as she exited the car. She reappeared minutes later and leaned into Jac's window, "How about I drive down Sunday and we'll have brunch?"

"Sounds good," Jac answered.

"Got to get my purse back," Gloria teased but was more interested in talking with Brian about Jac's health. She kissed Jac and wished her a safe trip home reminding her to call when she arrived.

Driving home, Jac's mind was filled with thoughts of her experience at Royal's. Mostly how the dresses looked so shapeless and her reflection appeared way too thin. She knew she would be seriously concerned for an animal if it came into the clinic with the same appearance issue.

"What could possibly be happening to me?" she asked aloud looking for answers.

When Jac arrived home, she quickly called Gloria, as had she requested, and thanked her for the wonderful day.

"I love you, Mom."

"I love you too, darling. See you Sunday. Have fun," Gloria responded.

Jac then called Brian with the good news and anxiously awaited his arrival. As soon as Brian entered the house, Jac pulled him into the living room to show him the dress spread out on the couch.

"Isn't it beautiful?" she exclaimed.

"I think it will be beautiful on you, pretty lady," he agreed. Brian was happy to see Jac had succeeded on her dress-hunting expedition and admired her selection knowing the blue would look great on her. At the same time, he was relieved the dress wasn't black, which would make her look even paler and malnourished, resulting in questions and the behind-the-back kind of talk he despised.

"Would you like to see it on?" Jac asked with enthusiasm.

"Yes, but not today. I can wait till Saturday. I know your mom wouldn't let you leave the store with anything that didn't look great on you."

Satisfied with Brian's answer, Jac gathered the dress and headed upstairs. Instead of hanging it in the closet, she chose to hang it on the back of the bathroom door, allowing the pleats to hang freely.

Days seemed to move slowly for Jac in anticipation of the big event. She was looking forward to an opportunity to mix and mingle with Brian's colleagues, plus the added bonus of dinner and dancing. The reception was to begin at five for the meet-and-greet, followed by a few words from the mayor. Everyone knew there would be a request to contribute to his campaign. It's the price expected to pay to attend the event. Dinner and dancing were scheduled to begin immediately following the mayor's speech and continue well into the night. Normally, Brian would shy away from such events, but since his boss was a good friend of the mayor, he was obligated to attend.

Brian continued to watch Jac's appetite improve, but not consistently, and he was determined to identify the cause of the irregularity.

Saturday morning, Jac sprang out of bed and hit the floor loud enough to wake Brian.

"Hey, sleeping here. It's Saturday. I get to sleep in," he muttered while pulling the pillow over his head.

"Good for you. I have clients to see and a party to get ready for." Jac quickly dressed and went downstairs to start breakfast. She knew the aroma of coffee brewing and bacon cooking would be more than Brian could stand.

"Ugh!" Brian threw off the pillow and headed downstairs. "You're not playing fair," he teased as he grabbed her close for a kiss.

Jac smiled and showed him to the table where she had a full plate of food and a hot cup of coffee waiting for him.

"So what's on your calendar today?' Brian asked in between bites.

"I have a few early appointments today and I'm closing the clinic at two. That should give me enough time to get ready for the ball."

"Well, in that case, I'll take care of the kitchen after I get in a quick run and mow the grass. Now go on to work and I'll see you this afternoon. Have a great day. Love you!" He kissed her goodbye.

Jac sped out the door and across the drive with more pep in her step than usual.

Brian loved seeing her enthusiasm and was looking forward to dancing with her in his arms. Together they made an attractive couple. He stood a few inches taller than Jac which he was grateful for when she wore heels. Her fair complexion and red hair were sharp contrasts to his tanned skin and black hair.

Brian ran every day and his tan was limited to what his shorts and tee-shirt wouldn't cover. His Spanish heritage made it easy for him to tan. Jac, on the other hand, would be outdoors the entire summer and not get a bit of color unless it was an occasional burn. Besides keeping fit, Brian ran as an outlet for stress. Lately, the stress was about Jac and trying to solve the weight riddle. He stood at the door and watched her go into the clinic before heading out for his run. After mowing, trimming, and removing the grass clippings, he was more than ready to jump in the shower. He was cleaning up the kitchen and sporting a pair of shorts when Jac came through the door.

"Hey, pretty lady. Is it quitting time?"

"Yes, it is. Have you cleaned up yet?" she asked hoping to have the bathroom all to herself.

"Yes, the bath is all yours. I know better than to get in your way." Then Brian followed her upstairs.

"So, how was your day?" he asked.

"Pretty much normal. How about yours?"

"Well, all was going pretty good on the run until I noticed the neighbor's goat had gotten out and seemed determined to head-butt me. I never ran so hard in my life to escape that darn goat. He must have stayed with me for a mile or so."

Jac began laughing from the closet, first a muffled giggle, and the more she thought about the scene Brian described the louder her laughter grew. By the time she had removed all of her clothes, she was holding onto her sides from laughing so hard.

Brian was offended by her lack of concern for his welfare, "I could have really been hurt by that darn goat."

Jac couldn't contain herself and slid onto the floor laughing holding her sides and wiping tears from her eyes. Brian watched Jac for a moment, naked, laughing on the floor and joined in, finally realizing just how funny it must have appeared.

Jac got back to her feet and embraced Brian. "Sorry you had a rough run, but that is the funniest thing I've heard in a long time. Glad you were able to outrun the goat and you're okay."

"Thanks. I guess looking back on it, it was pretty funny," Brian said.

"I have to get busy if I'm ever going to be ready in time. Thanks for the laughs." Jac kissed Brian. Then, enjoying the view, Brian watched Jac dance into the bathroom.

Jac took extra time in the shower, wanting everything to be perfect. Steam had rolled out of the shower and into the bedroom when she finally emerged.

"Hot enough for you?" Brian said coming out of the bedroom and grabbing a towel. Jac was pink from the heat of the shower and her hair was a mass of ringlets circling her face. Brian thought she was the most beautiful woman he had ever seen as he wrapped the towel around her and kissed her.

"Whoa now, big fella. I know what you're thinking and that is not in the plan right now. Later, I promise." Reluctantly, Brian retreated back to the bedroom and began getting his tuxedo together.

Jac waited for the steam to clear before doing her hair. Always the easiest part, thick and naturally curly, she didn't need to do much to it. She had decided to wear it down tonight so a quick blow dry would do the trick. Jac didn't wear much makeup and rarely applied anything more than moisturizer and sunscreen on a daily basis. Tonight, she was going all out with the whole arsenal. Jac applied her makeup as carefully as an artist. Not too much, but just enough for her to feel and look beautiful for Brian.

When Jac emerged from the bathroom, she took Brian's breath away. He couldn't believe how a person who looked as beautiful as she did earlier could appear even more beautiful now. He whistled a long catcall and Jac blushed in appreciation. "You're absolutely gorgeous. I'm a lucky guy."

"Why thank you, kind sir. I find myself pretty lucky to be with your handsome self, too."

"But I'm not finished." She lifted the dress off the hanger and slipped it over her head, careful not to mess up her makeup. "Now all I have left is my shoes."

Brian moved into the bathroom to finish getting ready. Dressed from the waist down Brian began brushing his teeth. Suddenly, there seemed to be a lot of stomping and cursing coming from the bedroom. With toothbrush in hand, Brian peeked around the corner. His mouth gaped wide at the sight of Jac in the closet pulling off the dress while complaining about how fat she was.

"I have to find something else to wear," she ranted.

Clothes flew out of the closet covering the floor, bed, lamps, and anything in the path of her tirade. Finally settling on a black skirt and baggy blouse, she walked over to view herself in the new mirror and adjusted the mirror's wings.

"This is way too baggy on me, why on earth would I wear this?" Jac tore off the skirt and blouse and once again put on the dress.

Satisfied the drama was over, Brian resumed brushing his teeth, only to hear Jac stomping and cursing once again. Brian moved to the doorway and witnessed Jac pulling the dress back over her head again shouting.

"Why does this dress make me look so fat? Why did I ever buy it?"

Brian had finally figured out the riddle and tossed the toothbrush at the sink.

"Wait, babe, let me help." His voice was quiet and supportive. "Let's take the shoes you want to wear and the dress over here so you can see it all together. I know you're going to like what you see." He led her out of the closet and over to where the large mirror stood.

"I doubt it. I saw what I looked like in there." She waved her arms towards the closet.

"Oh, Brian, I think I'm not going to be able to go tonight." Tears filled her eyes. Brian knew he had to do something fast.

He pleaded with Jac to once again put on the dress and said, "Stay right here. I'll be right back."

"Back? Wait, where are you going?" Jac asked.

"Just trust me." Descending the stairs to the kitchen, Brian rummaged through the junk draw and found the hammer. Racing back to Jac, he took the stairs two at a time and was breathless when he reached her.

"What are you doing?" But Brian was on a mission and didn't have time to stop. He marched into the closet and made quick work of removing the mirror. Jac watched Brian and waited on their bed, sitting in the dress.

"I am saving you from a distorted truth!" Brian declared as he set the closet mirror against the wall in the hall.

"What are you talking about?"

"Jac, please put on your shoes and take a look at yourself in the mirror."

"Which one?" she asked, totally confused.

"Your birthday present, so you can see your full reflection"

"Well, okay," she reluctantly agreed, "but I don't think it is going to change anything." Jac put on her shoes and stood in front of the mirror. "Oh!"

Brian walked up behind her and circled her waist. "You look absolutely beautiful and don't you ever forget it."

Jac nodded and for the first time in a very long time she liked her reflection and smiled at the woman looking back at her. "That mirror," he said, pointing toward the one he had just removed from the closet door, "was not reflecting the real you. It had you believing things about yourself that are untrue. This beautiful lady is the true you. I'm taking that lying mirror to be disposed of tomorrow. But tonight, we party!"

Brian quickly ran downstairs with the closet mirror and set it outside with the trash cans. He then sprinted back upstairs to finish dressing and found Jac exactly where he had left her.

Standing in front of the winged mirror, she asked, "How could this be? Two mirrors reflecting so differently. I don't understand it."

Brian walked over to her. "I don't know but this mirror has saved your life. We are so lucky to have found it when we did."

Brian finished dressing while Jac corrected the recent events' impact on her hair and makeup. She grabbed her sparkly crystal purse. "I'm famished. Let's go. Sure don't want to miss out on the appetizers."

"You go ahead, I'll be right behind you." Brian turned to address the mirror, not looking at his reflection but appreciating its warmth and beauty. "Thank you," he said aloud.

Just then, light reflecting through the bay windows caused the mirror to radiate a soft glow. Brian stepped back and stood in awe while witnessing the entire room fill with glowing light before turning and following after Jac.

Chapter 5

I was caught up in thoughts, hoping the mirror would sell quickly as I opened the door to Ruby's. I was greeted with the scent of fresh coffee and breakfast food cooking on the grill.

I took a seat at the counter, and Ruby gave me a big smile and nod that she would be with me soon.

Rounding the end of the counter Ruby said, "Hey, handsome. So good to see ya. What ya'll having today?"

"Hi, Ruby. I'll have the hungry man's breakfast, scrambled, with a cup of coffee, please."

"Sure thing." She turned over the cup and poured the coffee. "How ya'll been lately?" she asked in a lower voice so no one could overhear.

"Getting along okay. Got Digger to keep me company, and I've been working on some projects lately."

"Good to hear you been keeping busy. It's good therapy," she said before she took off with the coffee pot, weaving between tables through the diner.

I looked around and saw Ed a couple of stools down. Ed owns the Fish and Game Sports store in town and occasionally umpires the softball and baseball games. We've known each other since we were both knee high to a grasshopper. We exchanged hellos and shook hands as he moved to a closer stool.

"Good to see you, Jim."

"Same here, Ed."

We talked about the latest fishing lures, the weather, and the approaching baseball season; but all conversation came to a halt when our plates were served.

"Man o' man, this is good! Thanks, Ruby!" was the last thing I said until my plate was cleaned enough to see my reflection. Satisfied and feeling fat as a tick, I paid the check and said goodbye to Ed and Ruby. I was heading back across the square towards my truck when Hil caught up with me.

"Jim, hold up there. Have you got any more of those mirrors?"

"I'm sorry, Hil, that was one of a kind, why?"

"You sure called it right, Jim. No sooner than I turned the open sign around this morning a young couple came in and we sold your mirror. Well, if you do decide to make any more, we would be pleased to sell them for you."

"Thanks, Hil, I appreciate that," I said while shaking Hil's outstretched hand. Before I headed home, I turned and walked back across the square to Fred's Butcher Shop for a celebratory T-bone steak to share with Digger.

Digger was happy to see me, as always, and very interested in the package tucked under my arm.

"Later, boy, this is for dinner." I knew Digger wasn't interested in the particulars; he just wanted the bone to hide somewhere on the property.

Chapter 6

The next morning, Digger and I set out early for another road trip and were back home before most people were out of bed. Digger had found more old wood, and I filled the bed of my truck to the top. The wood was much larger than the last load and it took everything I had to get it into the truck. No sooner than the wood was unloaded and stacked in the shop the voice returned. This time the voice was deeper and more masculine. I wondered if this was always going to be the way with the reclaimed wood Digger and I found. I had learned my lesson with the first go-around and decided to trust this voice as well, to guide and direct me through the process.

Once stripped, sanded, and planed, the beauty of the hickory hidden under a layer of decay came to life. The first instruction from the voice was to use the largest pieces and turn out baseball bats on the lathe. This was a new experience for me, and I listened to every detailed word of instruction from the voice. Fortunately, I had experience working on the lathe making table and chair legs. There weren't many pieces of wood large enough to fulfill the request and not much room for error. I decided to do a test run of the settings and directions on an old pine four-by-four I had in the shed.

Pleased the pine bat turned out perfect, I felt confident enough to proceed with the hickory. Concentrating on the precision and measurements used on each piece of wood, I was able to get ten bats turned without any issues. I stepped back and admired the results. However, the voice wasn't ready to quit there.

"Now what?" I asked aloud. I have made ten bats for a team that doesn't exist. "This will be interesting." I said and looked over at Digger lying by the door. Digger's only response was a thud, thud, thud of his tail wagging against the floor.

There was a lot of wood left after making the bats, and I knew there were going to be more instructions. The shop was littered with a large amount of wood chips and sawdust. I started up the vacuum to get after the mess and prepare the shop for whatever the voice had planned next. But before I could get very far, the voice returned. As I suspected, we weren't finished. The next project was to turn drumsticks on the lathe.

"Drumsticks, what on earth would I do with a bunch of drumsticks?" I said aloud back to the voice.

This sounded even crazier than the baseball bats. Having learned to listen to the voice, I resigned myself to making drumsticks.

The work on the lathe went well into the early morning hours of the next day, and I hadn't been aware of how long the process had taken as time seemed to disappear. I finally looked up after the last drumstick was removed from the lathe and counted twenty drumsticks in total of all shapes and sizes. A small wedge of bright yellow and red beneath a silvery blue bank of clouds appearing on the horizon surprised me when I opened the shop's doors.

"Well, boy, guess we better get some shut-eye; or is it breakfast first and then some sleep?"

Digger got excited at the mention of breakfast and made mad dashes between me and the house until we reached the kitchen door.

"Okay, breakfast it is." I poured his kibble and refreshed his water dish. A bowl of cereal, for me, easy and quick. I jumped into the shower and enjoyed the refreshing hot water on my face as it washed away the wood dust. I closed all the blinds, making the room as dark as possible before going to bed. Digger settled in his usual place alongside my back and that was the last thing I remember before drifting off to sleep.

Sometime around noon, I was shaken awake by Digger anxiously jumped on and off the bed.

"Time to get up, boy?" His whine was all I needed to know it was time for Digger to go out. Still feeling a bit on the rough side, I stumbled into the kitchen.

"Here you go," I said opening the door. I then turned toward the coffee maker and started a full pot. My head was still in a fog and I needed all the help I could get to wake up and focus.

After a while, I made my way back to the shop and sanded the bats and drumsticks to a baby-butt smooth finish. Ten bats and twenty drumsticks took more time than I would have thought, but I knew attention to detail was necessary for a quality finished product. The remainder of the day was spent cleaning up shavings and sawdust in the shop from the sanding and the lathe marathon. Determined to get to bed at a reasonable time, I gave each piece a final wipe of the tack cloth and called it a day. Digger seemed ready to head back to the house as well, and we both trudged up the walk, hungry and exhausted.

The next day the voice instructed that labels had to be done on the face grain of the bats before they could be varnished. Baseball players know not to hit on the label or 180 degrees opposite due to the possibility of breaking the bat. I fired up my wood burner and each bat received an oval outline with "Libertyville, LA" in the center. Satisfied with the artwork, I cleaned the shop. As far as I was concerned, I was done for the day.

I ignored the remaining wood and probable future projects the voice had in store for me and decided, after the last couple of demanding days, Digger and I needed some R&R. I headed toward the shed with determination and grabbed my fishing tackle. Digger was hot on my heels, knowing exactly where I was headed. We walked a well-worn path through the tall grass. I had walked down this path so many times over the years I could probably do it with my eyes closed. Digger would usually walk alongside me for a while, then nudge me for an ear rub before taking off in a zigzag pattern down the path. He'd keep his nose to the ground, running from one rock, patch of grass, or root cropping to another. He was good company and always brought a smile to my face with his antics. I stepped into the clearing and stood for a few minutes, took a deep breath, and appreciated the view. Old trees surrounded the lake and provided much-needed shade, especially during the summer months. Sun filtered through the trees causing the lake surface to sparkle like diamonds. A rope swing still hung off a large branch over the swimming hole. It looked inviting. I shook my head and smiled, remembering some of the crazy stunts the guys and I had done off that rope swing and had lived to tell about it.

A bubbling spring kept the lake fed, and it sounded like music to my ears. Digger loved the water but had a love-hate relationship with the bubbling water of the spring. Determined to catch the water as it bubbled, he would bite at it each time it rose to the surface until it caught him by surprise and gushed up his nose. Eventually soaked and exhausted, he'd leave the spring to fight another day.

Digger climbed out of the water, shook and then came over to me for an ear rub. He stretched out in the sun and took a nap while I continued to cast. I wasn't really interested in catching any fish, just enjoying some peace. We stayed at the lake until my stomach growled and reminded me it had been a while since breakfast. I whistled for Digger and headed back up the path to the house.

I returned to the shop the next day and felt pretty good. A trip to the lake always restored my mind and energy. The bats and drumsticks both required the same finishing touches. It never occurred to me before how similar the two were in their production. I applied varnish, sanded, and repeated over the following days until the voice was satisfied with results.

The voice returned the next day with instructions to take the remaining hickory and make easels. With the help of the voice, I was able to determine two easels would be possible: one could hold a large picture of at least sixty inches wide and the other could display smaller pictures of thirty-six inches or less. The adjustable supports for the pictures made the easels versatile. Wood for the easels—like the mirror and the bats—was cut, sanded, and varnished; and I was careful to apply just the right amount of varnish as to not make the movements of the easel stiff. Assembly would have to wait until I went to Ray's for the hardware.

Chapter 7

My shop, which once provided furniture-making space only, now contained ten bats, twenty drumsticks, and two partially finished easels; there was no more room or hickory wood left. I surveyed the results of the past weeks, wondering why these items were chosen by the voice. I didn't have to wait very long to find out. My cell phone began ringing and broke my train of thought.

"Hello?" I said, half expecting another robocall.

"Hi, Jim, this is Ed."

"Hi, Ed, what's up?"

"Jim, everyone knows the Liberty Stars baseball team has not had a winning season for the past few years, and I'm calling around for donations to buy the team new equipment. I'm hoping it will boost the kids' morale and confidence. Can I put you down for a donation?"

I was stunned and silent for a short time while I digested what Ed had just asked me.

"Ed, I do have something to donate for the team. Would you be able to meet me this Saturday morning at Ruby's?"

"You got a deal. Breakfast is on me. See ya'll Saturday."

I hung up the phone and looked down at Digger. "Well, boy, that answered the question about the bats." Digger's response was the usual thump, thump, thump of his tail.

The phone call from Ed was perfect timing. Saturday I would be able to donate the bats to the high school baseball team, enjoy a free breakfast, and get the hardware needed to complete the easels. I should have known not to question the voice, but I'm only human and still had my doubts.

Digger and I made a trip to the lake every day the rest of the week and caught up on sleep.

Saturday morning, I loaded up the truck with bats and headed into town to meet up with Ed.

Ed was one of the rope-swing guys; we could tell tales on each other for days. His adventurous personality matched the boldness of his red hair. There wasn't a dare he wouldn't take on. He was a great guy to have in your corner, always happy to help anyone in need and support a good cause. The Libertyville High School baseball team was his current cause, and I was only too happy to help.

Ed was waiting for me when I pulled up at Ruby's.

"Hey buddy!" I said while shaking Ed's outstretched hand and patting his back.

"Hey yourself. I want to thank you for helping out the team."

"Glad you called me. You won't believe what I have for the team." I replied.

"Really, show me," he said peeking over the bed of the truck. "What ya'll got back there, a body?"

"No, now wait a minute. I believe you said something about buying me breakfast." I reminded him. We laughed and headed into Ruby's. After we each had our fill, we were back looking in the truck bed, and I was pleased to see the puzzled look on Ed's face when I dropped the tailgate.

"Still don't have a clue of what's in here?" I said.

"Nope, and I don't have all day to spend on a guessing game with you," he replied.

I pulled back the tarp and exposed the carefully wrapped cargo.

"Bats, where did you get bats?"

"I made them."

"Never knew you knew how to make bats," Ed said, eyeing me suspiciously.

"I was able to get my hands on some good hickory wood and was inspired to make bats; and, as luck would have it, you are in need of some," I replied avoiding eye contact. "Swing one around and let me know what you think."

Ed pulled one of the bats out of the truck and checked around to make sure it was safe before he wound up and swung the bat. He let out a low whistle, which I took as a compliment.

"They not only look good but they're well balanced."

"Thanks, I hope it helps bring the team good luck and lots of runs."

"Me, too. How many ya got in here?" Ed was already grabbing the bats and loading them into his trunk.

"Made ten. That's all the wood I had," I said, handing Ed the last bat.

"The first game is next Saturday. Come watch them play and see how these bats of yours work out."

"Looking forward to it. What time?"

"Four at the big diamond," he said backing out.

I waved bye to Ed and went on over to Ray's Hardware for the items needed to finish the easels.

Chapter 8

I loved going into Ray's about as much as Ruby's. Ray's Hardware had or could get just about everything one would need to repair or build anything. I could get lost for hours going up and down the store aisles, fantasizing about possible projects with each item that caught my eye. Ray greeted me at the sound of the bell above the door—every shop around the square had one.

"Jim, my good man. It's good to see you! Are you just looking around or interested in something particular today?"

"Both, but mostly I'm here to pick up a few items I need to finish a project," I replied.

"Call out if you need any help."

"Thanks, Ray."

I headed down the aisle determined not to get sidetracked. I was successful in finding everything I was looking for, which is typical in Ray's. I had been there so often I knew the store layout just about as good as Ray did.

Checking out, I noticed a flyer sitting on the counter for another Libertyville High School fundraiser.

"Hey, Ray, what's this about?"

"They are trying to raise money for the band and music department with a dinner and silent auction over at the church in a few weeks.

"I think they want to buy new instruments," he replied.

I looked at Ray dumbfounded and at the same time thought to myself, this was no coincidence. I knew exactly where the ten pair of drumsticks would be going. I paid for the hardware and grabbed one of the flyers. As soon as I got home, I went into the shop, dropped off the hardware, and studied the easels for a bit. It suddenly dawned on me all of the hickory wood had been used and the voice was gone. Somewhat saddened by the realization, and at the same time relieved, I walked up to the house and made a call to Lauren Ledbetter.

Lauren was the music director at Libertyville High and the flyer had identified her as the person to contact for more information. Excited to get my call and a donation for the band, she suggested we meet at Ruby's for breakfast next Saturday. I agreed and thought I wasn't sure what the future held for delivering the hickory easels, but these Ruby's breakfasts were eventually going to catch up with my waistline.

Monday, I made another trip into Ray's and bought some wood. Hil had called and said a customer was looking for a maple entrance table. I often made custom orders for H&E and was grateful for the work. In the following days, while working on the table, I would catch myself listening for a voice, but none came. The table was completed before the week was out, and I made arrangements with Hil to bring it by the store Saturday morning before meeting with Lauren.

Lauren was a pretty lady and, unless you already knew, you'd never guess her age. Keeping pace with the high school and church music programs seemed to agree with her. Lauren moved to town about three years ago. I had heard she was originally from New Orleans. Since coming to Libertyville, she has been in the middle of anything pertaining to music in town. When Lauren smiled, her blue eyes sparkled and her pink lips parted into what appeared as pearls nestled in a rosebud. You couldn't help yourself but to smile back. After delivering the table to H&E, I spotted her standing outside of Ruby's.

When I crossed the square, she smiled and said, "Hello there, Jim. I was so glad to get your phone call the other day. What a pleasure, yes, a pleasure indeed."

"Thank you. You're as bright and cheery as the sun today, Miss Lauren."

"Jim, you're going to make me blush."

I opened the door for us to enter and Ruby spotted us right off.

"Be with you two in just a minute. Go ahead and find yourselves a table."

We settled into a booth next to the door and chatted about the weather, the fundraiser, and anything else to avoid the uncomfortable sideways glances we were getting from the other customers.

After we ate, I paid for breakfast and helped Lauren with her chair. We exited Ruby's, both heaving a sigh of relief.

"Well, that was fun. Show me what you have for the band, and it had better be good after that experience," Lauren said.

We both laughed.

"I'll be right back. It's in my truck parked over at H&E."

I moved the truck over to Ruby's next to Lauren's car and pulled the drumsticks out of the cab.

"Oh, Jim, these are beautiful drumsticks. Where on earth did you buy these?"

"I made them," I found myself saying with a little too much pride in my voice.

"You made these? How did you know the band needed new drumsticks?" she asked as she balanced a drumstick on her fingertip.

I found answering these types of questions without sounding like a complete idiot was getting harder and harder each time.

"I was using some hickory wood for another project, had some left over and decided to give it a shot." I said, opening her car door and hoping my explanation didn't sound lame.

Lauren got into her car. "Well, Jim, I'm impressed. The kids are going to love them. Thank you."

"You're welcome. Take it easy," I said, closing her car door.

"I hope to see you at the fundraiser," she called as she backed out and waved goodbye.

Two out of three, I said to myself as I climbed into the truck. Funny, I would have never thought things would have turned out this way. I love Ruby's but sure hope the easels didn't involve another Saturday breakfast, I thought, laughing to myself. I started backing up when I was sure I heard someone call out my name. I stopped and pulled back in, shifted into park, and shut off the engine. Recent voice events made me stop and listen not knowing if what I heard was real.

Ethel's face appeared in my rearview mirror walking with sincere determination toward my truck.

"Hello, Ethel. Was that you calling my name?" I said, smiling as I opened my door for a hug.

"Yes, I hope you're able to help us with a customer's special request," she said a little breathless.

"I'll give it my best shot. What can I do for you?"

"We have been asked to locate a couple of good sturdy wooden easels for the gallery shop owner."

Stunned, I looked at Ethel for a few seconds before I was able to give her an answer.

"Ethel, I think I have just what you're looking for. I have just finished two real nice hickory easels. One would hold a large picture up to sixty inches; the smaller one adjusts up to thirty-six inches."

"Perfect, when can we expect to get delivery?"

"Would Monday morning work for you?"

"Yes. Thanks, Jim. You're the best. I got to run back to the store before Hil gives everything away." She turned and sprinted back across the square with a bit of a skip here and there.

H&E had big windows and a good view of the square. Ethel pretty much knew all who's, what's, and where's of the town square, so it didn't surprise me much when she had appeared at my truck out of the blue. Still shaking my head in amazement of the recent events, I started the engine and headed for home.

The hardware from Ray's was the perfect functional and finishing touches. The trick with the easels was to make them attractive and sturdy without overpowering the pictures displayed. Satisfied with the results after testing the easels' ability to be adjusted for various picture sizes, I cleaned up the shop and headed for the house to get ready for the game.

Chapter 10

I showered and shaved while wondering if the bats would be used and if they would make a difference to the team's performance. Five years of being at the bottom of the rankings was hard for the team's moral. "Libertyville losers" was often chanted by the opposing teams, making things worse; and it didn't take long to see the team's morale drop.

When I left for the ballgame, I told Digger goodbye, reassuring him I would be back later. He was given instructions to watch the house and be good till I got back. I shouted out the window to him "and no parties or girls" as I turned the truck toward the Libertyville baseball fields.

The town supported and appreciated the Libertyville school teams. Most everyone supported the New Orleans Saints, but there wasn't much in the way of entertainment or sports to be found around town outside of the school's activities. A few years back, the old house next door to the school was torn down and the land was donated to the school. After much debate and deliberation of what to do with the property, it was agreed to build dedicated baseball and softball fields with bleachers, an announcer's booth, concession stand, and lights. Fortunately, the property was large enough to accommodate more than one field, which came in handy during little league games.

Admission to the games cost five dollars and helped pay for the maintenance of the fields. A local grounds maintenance crew volunteered to keep the fields in top condition for half of the admission revenues.

At the ticket booth, I paid the five dollars and quickly hit the concession stand for a couple of hot dogs, nachos, and a drink. Balancing my purchases, I made my way over to the bleachers and spotted Ray and his wife, Pat.

"Got the necessities I see," Ray said.

"Can't go to the game without taking advantage of the best hot dogs in town," I replied while maneuvering onto the bench. "Evening, how are you?"

"We are really good. It's beautiful weather for a ballgame," Pat answered.

The players were already warming up and everyone was hoping for a better season. When Lauren entered the field, all activity ceased and we all stood while she sang the national anthem. Her voice was perfect and could hit even the high notes. I was amazed.

Ray took notice and elbowed me in the ribs, "Close your mouth before something flies into it!"

Suddenly aware I was still standing and staring at Lauren, I noticed giggling coming from Ray and Pat as they observed my obvious infatuation. Lauren left the field and looked around for a place to sit in the stands. Ed yelled, "Play ball!" and the players took the field. I stood up and waved for Lauren to join us. She spotted me and nodded in agreement. Lauren made her way to our row and everyone shifted a little more in one direction on the bench.

"Hello, and thank you for making room," she said openly to everyone within earshot. Hellos were exchanged back, and then everyone turned their attention toward the field and the Libertyville Stars.

The events that took place on the field, and more importantly the batter's box, were just short of miracles. The coach insisted the team use the new wood bats instead of the aluminum bats they had been using. The Liberty Stars succeeded in hitting the ball every time they came to the plate. Singles, doubles, and even home runs were being hit by every player on the team. It didn't take much to notice the whole team had a new confidence. Catches were made, balls were smacked, and the runs were adding up. Everyone was hoarse from all the cheering and yelling going on. The Stars had started the season with a winner and everyone was in the mood to celebrate.

"Is anyone up for an ice cream at the Creamery?" I asked the group.

"Absolutely!" came in a resounding response.

"We're thinking alike," Ray said with a big smile and pats on my back.

"You buying, since it was your idea?" he continued.

"Sure, Ray, I'll get the first round if you get the next." We both laughed as we walked toward the parking lot.

Chapter 11

The Creamery had been a local hangout for years. People would drive from all over Red River Parish to get Creamery ice cream. Everything on the Creamery menu was homemade, using milk, eggs, and other ingredients from local farmers.

We all agreed to ride in one car because parking could be a nightmare at the Creamery on a Friday night. Confident that we were not the only ones at the game with the same idea, we all piled into Ray's SUV. Secretly, I was happy to be able to sit next to Lauren and hoped no one noticed. I caught myself looking at her and was drawn into wanting to know her better. Inside the Creamery, we recalled great plays of the game while we ate our ice cream. We made fun of ourselves recalling our enthusiastic and somewhat obnoxious cheering, hooting, and hollering for the Stars.

The evening ended on an even higher note after the Creamery. Ray returned us to the parking lot at the ball field, and we said good night to Ray and Pat, leaving Lauren and me alone in the deserted parking lot. We continued to talk while leaning on Lauren's car. She and I lost all track of time until the church bells rang out twelve times.

"Oh, is that the time? I have to be going home. I have choir tomorrow. I hope I'll be able to sing after all the yelling and cheering I did at the game."

Reluctantly, I agreed to call it a night. We awkwardly hugged each other and said goodbye. I walked back to my truck and drove the entire way home smiling, remembering every detail of the evening.

I hadn't thought about Judy the entire evening, but as I pulled into the drive, thoughts of her flooded my mind. Feeling somewhat guilty for being attracted to another woman, I decided to give myself some distance from Lauren for a while.

I delivered the easels to H&E Monday morning, as I had promised Ethel, and avoided the temptation of a Ruby's breakfast. The Stars' game was the talk of the town everywhere I went. From the gas station to the grocery store, people were excited for the team and anticipated another win at the next game. The losing streak had been broken; no more having to listening to the Libertyville loser chants and taunts. One winning game doesn't make for a winning season, but everyone agreed the Stars were already ahead of their record of the last five years. I was careful and quick to avoid running into Lauren.

Lauren was a great women, and I was sure she didn't have a clue on why I hadn't gotten back in contact with her. I was at a loss for words because I was dealing with difficult emotions and loyalties to Judy. I knew the fundraiser for the band was next week, and I needed to figure it out before seeing Lauren again. I owed her an apology and explanation. I just didn't know how to explain to her what I was going through. I needed to make a decision to either live in the past with memories of Judy or make new ones with Lauren.

Chapter 12

The next day I stopped the riding mower in the middle of the front lawn and took a long look at the farmhouse making the decision right there and then about what would be my memorial addition. Every carpenter in the family had made their mark on the farmhouse and mine was soon to be included. I began making plans to expand the front porch to wrap around from one side to another and add a screened-in porch across the back. I imagined it would be a great place for Digger and me to enjoy sunsets over the lake. A big undertaking, I knew, but in my mind's eye, the house would be more relaxing and inviting. An added bonus would be shade over the first-floor windows and back door, reducing heat from the summer sun.

I called Ray and told him of my plans for the house. Knowing he wouldn't have the amount of lumber I needed, I asked him to order everything on the list I gave him and have it delivered to the house. Delivery would cost a little more, but it was worth not having to make multiple loads from a big box store in the city.

Besides, I like to support the businesses around town, especially Ray's.

Ray ordered the lumber and supplies and called back with an expected delivery date.

"That is a lot of work, Jim. Call me when you can use an extra hand, I'll be glad to help." Ray volunteered.

"Will do," I said grateful for his offer.

I got real busy real fast making ready for the new additions. The rose bushes originally planted by my mother were dug up and carefully set aside to be added back later. I checked and rechecked measurements and prepared the house for expansion. The porch project kept me busy for quite a while, and I enjoyed being outside absorbed in the project, not thinking too much about Judy or Lauren.

The fundraiser day arrived and I was prepared to see Lauren again. I wasn't certain she had the same feelings about me, but I had made up my mind to find out. We needed to talk, and I knew tonight would not be the right time. I had to ask Lauren for a date. I had never asked a girl for a date before. Judy and I were always friends. Our relationship never got that formal until I asked her to marry me. Communication was easy; at times it seemed she could read my mind. I'm sure she knew I was going to propose long before I did.

When I entered the fundraiser in the church gym, I noticed Lauren right off the bat. She looked prettier than the last time I saw her. At first, I didn't want her to know I was there so I could stand back and watch her for a while. She must have felt me staring at her. She turned toward my direction and sent me a smile that calmed my fears about her feelings. I smiled and nodded back and waited for her to make her way through the crowd.

"Hello, stranger," she said when she got close enough.

"Hello, yourself. You look prettier each time I see you," I replied. "I owe you an explanation of why you haven't heard from me, but this isn't the time or place. Would it be okay if I called you tomorrow so we could arrange a time to meet and talk?" I asked, hoping my voice wasn't shaking as much as my insides.

"Sure, Jim. Call me anytime. Come on over here, I saved you a place at a table with Ed, Ray and Pat, and Hil and Ethel. You can be Ed's date since I'm crazy busy with everything going on here."

I laughed and nodded, relieved she had reserved a spot at a table with people I knew.

I enjoyed the meatball and spaghetti dinner and bid on a few of the silent auction items but didn't win any of them. Feeling the effects of working on the house, I was the first one at the table to excuse myself and offer everyone a good night. As I rose to leave, a slight groan escaped. Ray and Ed were both quick to tease me in unison.

"Getting old there, buddy?"

"Appears so, and to make it worse, it's past my bedtime." I answered over my shoulder as I headed toward the door.

When I called Lauren the next day, she invited me to her house for dinner Monday evening. I was nervous knowing this was a big step for me but, at the same time, relieved our conversation would be kept private. I stopped by Magnolia's for a bouquet of flowers and rang the doorbell precisely at six. Lauren quickly opened the door as a beautiful smile filled her face.

"Are those for little ole me?" she said batting her eyelashes and emphasizing her southern drawl.

"Yes, they are, little lady," I replied in my best impression of John Wayne. We both laughed and she invited me in.

"Have a seat at the table. Dinner is ready. Would you like something to drink? Your choices are beer, water, iced tea, or lemonade."

"That's quite a variety. Lemonade please."

Lauren had made a pot roast for dinner and when I finished I realized how much I missed home cooking.

"Lauren, dinner was delicious."

"Would you like more?" she offered.

"No, thank you. I draw the line at seconds. I am going to help you with the dishes and then we can sit down and talk, if that is okay with you?"

"How about we talk and do the dishes at the same time," she replied.

"I like the sound of that," I said.

After clearing the table, I started hand washing the dishes. Lauren offered to dry and then was silent, letting me take the lead on the conversation.

"Lauren, I want you to know how much I enjoy your company and would like to see you more often."

"You mean like date?" she asked.

"Yes, date, you and me."

"Okay," Lauren responded. "So was tonight our first date?"

"Sure, we could say that."

Glad the hardest part was over, I continued. "I needed to stay away for a while and work out some emotional stuff." I realized I had been scrubbing a pot a little longer and harder than necessary.

"That's what I thought," Lauren said as she laid her hand on my arm.

I turned to look in her eyes and leaned over to kiss her at the same time that she reached up and pulled my neck down. We met half way for a long deep kiss. Much later, the dishes were finished. We talked for hours until I realized that, the next day, Lauren would have to get up early.

"As much as I'm enjoying this evening, I think it would be best if I went home and let you get some rest," I offered.

"I know you're right, but I didn't get a chance to tell you about the drumsticks," she said.

"We can talk about the drumsticks when I call you tomorrow." We kissed good night and I drove home in a fussy fog.

The next morning, it didn't take long to see what Digger had been up to while I was gone. New holes were everywhere I looked. I made a mental note for safety sake to fill the holes in the driveway first. As I walked the property and reviewed the damage, I could tell Digger was proud of his work as he pointed out each hole. Unfortunately, I wasn't paying enough attention and stepped backward into one of his creations, ending up on my butt in the bottom of one of the larger craters. Digger took advantage of me being on the ground and began filling my face with big wet kisses. I wasn't hurt and laughed at his attempt to apologize.

Pushing him away and getting out of the hole began a game, and we wrestled on the lawn. Before it ended, we were covered in dirt, mud, grass, and slobber, exhausted and grinning from ear to ear. A man and his dog getting dirty and having fun, something we both enjoyed and hadn't done for quite a while.

The dirt and all didn't bother me much, and I chuckled as I brushed at my pants and we walked back up to the house. I then got started on the next phase of the new porch construction and worked until my stomach growled, reminding me to get something to eat. Late afternoon, I put a quick sandwich together and picked up the phone to call Lauren. When she answered, I could tell by her voice she was happy to hear from me.

"Hello there. I was wondering when I would be hearing from you today," she said. "What have you been doing?"

"Digger and I had a wrestling match on the front lawn and then I went to work on the house."

"What are you doing to your house, Jim?"

"I'll show you when I'm finished." I didn't want to tell Lauren what I was doing to the house thinking it would be fun to surprise her.

"So tell me what is going on with the band practices?" I said changing the subject.

Lauren went on to explain she was working hard to get the high school's marching band ready for the big Fourth of July Parade. She was very proud of the progress the band was making, and it's what mostly occupied our conversation. In past years, the rhythm section of the band wasn't worth their salt and couldn't keep a steady beat. Lauren went on and on about how they had improved and attributed the turnaround to the drumsticks and practice.

"A good drum section can make or break a band," Lauren explained. "We have been practicing the patriotic music and doing some simple street formations for the parade. I can hardly wait for the town to see their progress, and it all started with your drumsticks." I could hear the excitement in her voice.

"I'd like to think the drumsticks played a part in the improvement of the band's performance, but I think it has more to do with your dedication and the band's commitment," I responded.

The next couple of months seemed to fly by. I worked on the porch almost every day and made a point to see Lauren as much as our schedules would allow. The porch completely wrapped around the entire house, and I was pleased with the results. After a final coat of paint, the house's personality changed from a plain farmhouse to a classic southern estate. Reconstruction of the flower-beds and new landscaping completed the new exterior appearance. The addition of the screened-in porch across the back of the house turned out to be another good decision.

Digger and I made it a practice to watch the sun go down over the lake almost every night. Digger enjoyed dozing on the porch and would move around the house from one side to another lying in the sun. I was proud of my contributions to the legacy of the house. But it didn't stop with the exterior.

I began taking on the inside. Not much had been changed on the inside for decades. As is, a walk through the front door would stir memories of my youth and growing up in the old house. Memories of Judy and me would also fill my mind. Like the time when Digger was a pup and attacked our Christmas tree. Judy was so concentrated on cleaning up the mess she didn't notice Digger was sneaking up behind her and removing everything she had put into the wastebasket. Judy finally caught the little guy red-handed and scolded him and then me for not telling her what Digger was up to. Most of the memories would bring a smile to my face. Then there were some that would bring a tear.

Cleaning up and preparing the inside for remodeling seemed to take longer than I had anticipated. I looked around one last time before removing pictures and moving furniture for what I had planned. Wallpaper was removed, walls were repainted, and the wooden doors, cabinets and trim finishes were sanded and given a fresh coat of varnish. I moved the old refrigerator into my shop and updated the kitchen, replacing all of the appliances.

To help support my home-improvement projects, I worked on special orders from H&E. I used up odds and ends of wood stored in the shed and occasionally made wooden pens, lazy Susans, and salt and pepper shakers, which were a big hit with tourists that visited the town square shops.

I left the hardest part of the house cleaning and restoration till the very last. Pushing through memories and tears, I boxed up Judy's things and took them to church for the yearly rummage sale. As luck would have it, Pastor Luke was out front cutting the church lawn when I pulled into the driveway. He was dressed for the job in blue jeans and a blue long-sleeve shirt with a big straw hat on his head that flopped as he rode the lawn mower. Our senior pastor had retired soon after Judy's death, and Pastor Luke was doing a fine job of filling his shoes. A younger man, if I was to guess, in his mid- to late-forties and slightly chunky. I thought to myself that the church ladies were keeping him well fed.

"Hi, Jim," he said as he turned off the lawn mower and approached the truck.

"Hi, Pastor Luke. I have some things to add to the rummage sale." I thumbed the boxes stacked in the bed of the truck. "Where do you want them?"

"Pull around back. There is a whole room in the Rec Center for contributions. It's on your right as you enter the back door," he directed. "Do you need some help?"

"No, sir, I got this," I replied.

"When you're done, come on up on the porch and I'll get us some lemonade," he said.

"Sounds good!" and I turned down the drive to unload the truck.

While closing the door to the Rec Center, I was once again overwhelmed with sadness and heartache. I still missed Judy and saying goodbye to her belongings I knew was a necessity, but that didn't make it any easier. My eyes were still watery when I met Pastor Luke on the porch.

"I'm guessing those boxes you brought were Judy's things; am I right?"

I nodded, afraid to talk, fighting back emotions and a large lump in my throat.

"It sure must have taken a lot of strength for you to pack it up. Is there anything you would like to talk about, Jim?" he said offering me lemonade.

I sat there a minute or two and gained my composure before answering.

"Yes, Pastor Luke. You probably know Lauren and I have been seeing quite a lot of one another." I hesitated as I organized my thoughts.

Pastor Luke nodded and waited patiently for me to continue.

"I'm concerned our relationship may be viewed as too much too soon after Judy's passing. You know the people of Libertyville love to talk, especially the ladies at the 2&4 Beauty Shop, and I wouldn't want anyone to think negatively toward Lauren."

Pastor Luke looked into my eyes and saw my concern and need for his advice. "Well, Jim," he began. "Judy passed two years ago and that is a respectable length of time for mourning. Lauren is a lovely, generous lady, and respected in this town for her talent and integrity. I believe any talk about you and Lauren at the 2&4 would be about how happy they are for you two."

He continued, "And if there is anyone out there who would talk negatively about either of you, they wouldn't be someone anyone of much worth would listen to. Jim, enjoy what you have together and know in your heart this is exactly what Judy would have wanted for you."

When the Pastor was finished speaking, we sat in silence for a while. I took a big drink of my lemonade and then a deep breath, relieved to get it off of my mind and heart.

"Thank you for the good advice and lemonade. You have helped me a great deal, Pastor. Now if you'll excuse me." I shook his hand and quickly started back to my truck.

I wanted to see Lauren and was hoping she would be home.

Lauren was busy with band, choir practices, and performances at the games. Lauren and I attended every game and the Liberty Stars were on a hot streak. No one wanted to mention it aloud for fear of jinxing it, but if the Stars kept it up, they would end up in the playoffs.

Lately, we had both been busy people, and I thought it would be a good idea if I called Lauren first before showing up unexpectedly at her door.

"Hello," she said.

"Where are you now?" I asked, anxious to see her.

"I'm home, looking over sheet music for Sunday. Why? Where are you?"

"Coming your way, I'll be there soon."

I hopped out of the truck and Lauren greeted me at the door.

"Well, this is a great surprise. I wasn't counting on seeing you until the weekend. What brings you into town, handsome?"

"I had to take care of some more details about what I've been doing around the house." I answered while stepping through the doorway.

"About that, when are you going to show me what you have been doing out there?"

"Well, that is why I'm here talking to you now. We've been so busy lately there didn't seem enough time to show you. Plus, there is something else, but it will have to wait until after the Fourth." I looked her into her eyes making sure her feelings weren't hurt.

I pulled Lauren closer and we kissed. When we parted, she set my mind at ease.

"Okay, I can wait until after the Fourth. It's not like the house is going anywhere. So you'll show me on the fifth?" she teased.

"Okay, it's a date. Hey, I know I interrupted your choir preparation, so I'll get out of your hair and call you later tonight," I said walking towards the door

"I'll see you tomorrow night at the church's Fourth of July committee meeting, right?"

"Sure," I answered. "Would you like to grab some dinner before the meeting? Otherwise, I fill up on coffee and desserts the ladies set out and end up staying awake half the night."

"I do, too. Dinner sounds like a good idea," Lauren answered.

"Great. I'll pick you up at five," I said and kissed her quickly before I exited through the door.

Driving home, I realized Lauren might have felt left out when I didn't include her in my plans for the house. She had a right to know there was more going on with me than just working on the house.

Chapter 14

It was clear the Fourth's celebration was going to make it harder for us to see one another.

Each Fourth of July celebration, committee members were asked to volunteer for an area to manage and work for the event. I jumped at the chance to set up and arrange the fireworks with Pastor Luke. Lauren, who already was working on music with the marching band, volunteered to coordinate the music for the fireworks show. She also volunteered to organize the cakewalk with donations from church members and Ruby's. My gal liked staying busy and I appreciated that about her.

We talked on the phone almost every night and shared the progress on each of our projects. I told her about traveling to Shreveport with Pastor Luke to purchase the fireworks and how much I learned about each type of display. I went on to explain the process of when and how to set the fuse timing for the fireworks to complement the music. I assured her that we bought the popular displays and also some new displays that promised to dazzle the crowd. In turn, Lauren shared her progress with the church ladies and their commitments to donate various desserts for the cakewalk. Ruby's was also on board with donations of their cherry, apple, and strawberry pies. Talking to Lauren about the cakewalk made my mouth water. I was already planning on participating in the cakewalk and hoped to win a sweet treat. We always said how much we missed each other, but neither one of us regretted our decision to volunteer. We knew when the Fourth's celebration was over, a date had been set to spend some important quality time together.

Before the Fourth, I spent a lot of time with Pastor Luke working out details of the fireworks show and doing some carpentry work around the church. I was not leaving much time for Digger and it showed. I arrived home one evening to find Digger sitting in the middle of the driveway with one of my fishing poles in his mouth. Fortunately for him, the hook caught in the frame of the shed. Unfortunately, for me the entire spool of line was strung out the full length of the driveway.

Digger bounded after me as I pulled up the drive. All the while, I watched the pole bounce off one tree after another in the rearview mirror. When I stopped the truck and got out, Digger dropped the pole at my feet and eagerly paced from me to the direction of the lake. I knew the pole was history the minute I saw it in Digger's mouth. I picked up what was left of the pole and gathered the fishing line as I made a mental note to put a lock on the shed door. But I got his hint.

The next day, Digger and I went down to the lake for a little "us" time. He wouldn't let me out of his sight and stayed close by while I fished, content to get his ears rubbed and hear some "good boys." I apologized for not being around too much. I told him how much I loved him and how much he meant to me. Digger laid down and listened with an occasional cock of his head to one side as I explained why I was away so much. When I stopped talking, Digger stood up, shook, gave me a sideways glance and was off like a flash to get after the bubbling water of the spring. Nothing had changed; the spring won again.

Soon Digger returned back by my side, wet and sneezing water. He shook the excess water off and looked at me with what appeared to be a devilish grin, knowing I was getting as wet as he was. We raced each other back to the house and, as always, Digger was the winner. He stood inside the screened-in porch, smiling back at me, proud of his success. He shook again, and I was thankful we had the sunporch in which to dry off without messing up the freshly painted kitchen.

Morning of the Fourth, Lauren must have called me at least a half dozen times making sure I was going to be in town at the right time, on the right street and the right corner, and reminding me not to forget my hat. I could tell she was excited and nervous about the band's performance.

"I don't want you to miss the new and improved Libertyville Marching Band," she said.

"Don't worry. I wouldn't miss it for the world."

Dressed in blue jeans, a red and white striped shirt, and sporting a new navy blue straw cowboy hat, I checked my reflection in the mirror and headed downstairs.

I called Digger into the house and shut the doggie door while I explained to him it was for his own good. There was going to be a lot of snap, crackle, and pops that evening.

The weather cooperated and attendance for the parade was high. I took my appointed place, sporting the hat Lauren suggested I wear so she could pick me out of the crowd.

I heard the music coming down the block and smiled to myself at how great they sounded. I was happy for her knowing how hard she worked to make their parade appearance a success. The mayor came first in a red convertible and waved while his wife threw candy into the crowd. The band followed, stopping every few blocks and stepping out of alignment, forming a star while playing "The Star-Spangled Banner," then moving into a flag formation playing "You're a Grand Old Flag." The crowd loved it. You could hear people all along the parade route clapping and singing along. After the band were a few homemade floats and people dressed as clowns. An array of dogs followed, mostly poodles, sporting patriotic colors dyed into their coats, courtesy of the 2&4 Beauty Shop. Some did tricks and amused the crowd. Everyone but the band threw candy, and the streets were lined with very happy kids retrieving and comparing their treasures. Finally, the fire department truck appeared, running its siren and signaling the end of the parade.

After the parade, various booths surrounding the town's square opened for business. Some offered the chance to win a prize, others displayed and sold their crafts and wares. The Fourth of July Celebration

Committee had insisted each booth was to be different and none of them were allowed to sell anything edible. While the celebration was on, the church was the designated place for something to eat and even Ruby's closed for the event. The Fourth was the church's big fundraiser for the year, and everyone, including the businesses, respected the event.

Traditionally, people from miles around would make Libertyville their go-to place to celebrate the Fourth. They would come for the festivities, the fireworks, and, most of all, the church's fried chicken and Fred's homemade brat dinners. The church meals were reasonably priced and many people would purchase one to eat there and one to take home.

I spotted Lauren at the cakewalk and could see she was having a great time with the event. After a successful parade, she was riding a happiness high and I was glad to be a part of it. I walked up and gave her a congratulatory hug while I tried not to get in the way of the cakewalk activities.

"What you've done with the band is amazing. Congratulations, I am very happy for you."

"Thank you. I couldn't have been more pleased with the results. The kids were terrific and everything went as smooth as glass," she said.

"I should be done here shortly. The pastries are going fast! If you want anything, you should get a ticket and join in."

"I do have my eye on those brownies over there. I'll be right back," I said and sped away to the ticket booth.

I bought quite a few tickets hoping to win something; but unfortunately, I wasn't very lucky at the cakewalk. When the event was over, Lauren came over and gave me a sympathetic smile and hug.

"Sorry you didn't win, but don't worry there's plenty of desserts at the church dinner."

I nodded as we made our way toward the square.

"There are more booths here than last year," I commented. "Guess the weather and all the publicity from the Stars' games have been helpful."

"I couldn't agree with you more," Lauren said.

I did much better at the game booths and was proud to present Lauren with a stuffed toy. We each bought a jar of honey from a local vendor and visited every booth around the square. Next up were the games at the football field. Anyone could participate and it was always loads of fun. We agreed to watch from the side-lines and cheered participants in one-legged races, relay races, raw-egg running races, and a water balloon toss contest. We laughed and rooted for people we knew.

Feeling a bit hungry, we followed the crowd over to the large tents set up in the church's parking lot. Tables were covered with plastic table cloths, and the chairs were a mixed-match donated for the event.

Lauren and I spotted Ray and Pat and Ed seated at a table and motioned for them to hold us a place. By the time we made our way through the line, Hil and Ethel had also joined the group. Greetings were exchanged, but conversations soon piddled out as everyone's appetite took over. I indulged myself with both a brat and chicken plate. Each meal included a drink, two sides, and your choice of a homemade dessert. After polishing off the dinners, I eyed the church ladies' homemade sweets displayed on the nearby table and suggested Lauren go with me to choose something. She looked surprised.

"Oh, no thank you, I'm as stuffed as I can be."

"I'm game," Ray joined in.

"Count me in, too," Hil said with a wink and grin at Ethel as he pushed away from the table.

"Would anyone like us to bring something back?" I asked the ladies at the table.

"A piece of coconut or lemon pie if they have any available," Ethel said.

Lauren and Pat shook their heads no.

Well, us guys don't always listen to our gals and we loaded up our arms with various pies, cakes, and cookies to bring back for the table. We carefully placed the desserts in the center of the table. The church ladies' sweets never disappoint and were a fine ending to the terrific meals. With everyone's appetite satisfied, conversation once again started up.

"Lauren, you have done a terrific job with the band. Last year, I couldn't even recognize some of the songs they played," Pat said.

"Thank you, Pat. I believe the new instruments gave the kids the confidence and desire to do their best."

"That and a lot of practice," I added.

"Hey, Ed, I have been keeping up with the Stars. Boy, they are really doing well this year," Hil said.

Ed nodded in agreement.

"We're taking one game at a time and trying not to jinx them by talking about their run of wins," Ray added.

"Now, that's another example of a group of kids getting new equipment and it changed their confidence. Come to think about it, it seemed to make a big difference when they started using those bats, Jim." Ed said.

"You know, Jim gave the percussion section new drumsticks, and I think that is why the rhythm section was able to turn the corner and maintain a steady beat," Lauren said to the group at the table.

Almost at the same time everyone's eyes turned towards me, and I adjusted nervously in my seat.

"As much as I would like to take credit for the improvements in the Stars and marching band, it really belongs to the coaches, Lauren and the kids. They're the ones who invested the long hours of practice and hard work," I said hoping to satisfy their curiosity.

Hil and Ethel looked up and waved to an attractive couple who approached the table pushing a baby stroller and I was grateful for their interruption.

"Hi, Brian and Jac," Hil said.

Brian nodded and replied "hello," while shaking hands with the guys within reach.

"Hi," Jac replied "Would anyone mind if I helped myself to that piece of chocolate cake?" She asked, eyeing the last dessert left in the center of the table.

"No!" was the resounding response.

"I'm glad you asked. Would you be willing to share it with me?" Brian asked

Jac nodded.

"I sure like eating sweets with you again," Brian said winking at Jac.

"How is this beautiful baby?" Ethel asked, carefully peeking into the stroller.

"Oh, she is doing great; as for us, well we could use a little more sleep," Brian answered.

Hil leaned over to me and shared, "That's the couple who bought your mirror. Looks like your special talents work in other areas, too."

"Oh no, Hil, I had nothing to do with making any babies!" I quickly responded.

Everyone within ear shot of us broke out in laughter.

"Okay, everyone, let's change the subject. I'm not the town hero. I'm only a carpenter that made a mirror, a few bats, and some drumsticks.

"Just saying, Jim, two may be a coincidence, but three makes a person think there may be more to it," Hil said giving me a suspicious look.

I didn't like where the conversation had gone and quickly made my exit, grateful for an excuse to leave.

"I would really like to stay and listen to more of your crazy theories, but I have to get going to the fireworks stand and help get this party started."

I kissed Lauren on her cheek and said, "I'll see you later, after the show."

Preoccupied in thoughts of the information revealed in the last few minutes, I ran right into Alex of Gallery A.

"Oh, I am so sorry, Alex. Are you okay?" I said as I helped him to his feet. I tower over Alex, and he ended up taking the brunt of our collision.

"I think so. Did you get the license number of the truck that just hit me?" he answered, a little shaky.

"No truck, just me not watching where I was going," I said.

"Where are you heading in such a hurry?"

"To help with the fireworks," I said.

"Me, too, I volunteered when I heard they were asking the shops to close at five today. The street lights will be turned off too, so it's nice and dark to see the fireworks. Pastor Luke announced at church last Sunday they could use some more volunteers and here I am."

"Great, how are you and the gallery making out lately?" I asked as we continued walking together.

Pretty good, actually. I purchased a set of easels from H&E a while back, and it's the craziest thing. Every picture I display on them sells within a week or two. The gallery specializes in promoting local artists and the increase of confidence and revenue has done wonders for them and the gallery."

I stopped walking alongside Alex and stared straight ahead at nothing.

"You okay, Jim? You look a little pale?"

Hearing my name brought me back to the present. I shook off the funny feeling rising from the pit of my stomach and continued walking as I offered Alex an explanation. "I'm okay, just having trouble with something I ate."

"It's so easy to do that at the church picnic. Every year I make a vow not to let my eyes get bigger than my stomach, but every year I eat way too much," Alex said.

The fireworks went up as planned and the "oohs" and "aahs" were plentiful. The music Lauren had arranged went perfectly with the fireworks display, and it all went off without one dud in the show. The finale noisily lit up the sky and was followed by an appreciative round of cheering and applause. The street lights came back on and everyone began making their way back to their cars and homes.

Lauren and I hung back and helped fold chairs and tables for Pastor Luke. We had had a great day and didn't want it to end; although, I could tell Lauren's energy was beginning to wane. I got involved helping the other volunteers break down the tents and lost all track of time. When I turned around to find Lauren, I spotted her resting on a bench leaning on one arm with her eyes closed.

"Time to go," I said softly in her ear.

Startled, she looked a bit embarrassed and nodded in agreement.

"It was the greatest Fourth ever! Everything was perfect, and I especially enjoyed sharing it with you," she said with conviction.

"That goes double for me," I said and kissed her before leading her to her car.

Just before she drove away, Lauren rolled down the window and reminded me of our date tomorrow.

"What time do you want me at your house?" she asked.

"I'll come pick you up at six. I want to watch your face when you see the house," I answered, thinking back on how much I would have liked to win a dessert at the cakewalk for tomorrow night's surprise.

Chapter 15

Early the next day, I decided to get more information about the easels from Alex. I was sitting outside of Gallery A when it opened.

"Hey, Alex," I called walking up behind him as he opened the doors to the gallery.

Alex jumped, "Oh, Jim, you startled me. Well, at least this time you didn't run me down."

"I'm interested in taking a look at those pictures you were talking about yesterday. You know the ones selling like hot cakes," I said.

"Sure, Jim, come on in."

We walked into the gallery and Alex directed me to the room where the easels were displaying two pictures.

"The same artist painted the pictures on the wall to your left, but it isn't until I set them on the easels that anyone even looks at them. Strangest thing. I can't figure it out. The lighting doesn't seem to make a difference or anything else, but for some reason the pictures sell quickly when displayed on the easels."

"Huh" was the only response I could come up with at the time.

I was happy the easels were doing so well for the local artists and Alex, but this added to my suspicion about the wood and the voices. I left the gallery and started back home after stops at Ruby's for an apple pie, Fred's for steaks and the Creamery for some vanilla ice cream.

Having a limited knowledge of cooking, I went with what I do best. The menu for the big reveal to Lauren was simple: steak, salad, baked potato, and to finish it off, apple pie and ice cream.

After cleaning and straightening inside and outside the house, I turned my attention to the dinner. The potatoes were washed; the salad was chilled; and the freezer was taking care of the ice cream. I set the pie on the counter and knew the steak and potatoes would be easy enough to finish off later. I looked around the kitchen making sure I didn't forget anything. Satisfied, I cleaned up and dressed for dinner.

I grabbed a towel from the linen drawer and planned to blindfold Lauren until she was in just the right spot on the drive, then say "surprise," as I undid the blindfold.

Lauren looked beautiful when she answered the door and I told her so. At first, she wasn't a big fan of the blindfold idea but eventually gave in and went along. Driving back to the house, I mentally checked and rechecked every detail of my plan for the evening, hoping Digger hadn't redecorated the front lawn and driveway with more holes before I got back with Lauren.

I pulled into the drive and parked in a spot far enough back for her to get a full view of the porch and landscape all at once. While I rounded the front of the truck, I watched Lauren for signs of peeking. I was convinced this wasn't the case when she stumbled getting out of the truck.

"This had better be worth it" was all I heard as I helped her regain balance.

"Surprise!" I gently removed the blindfold and waited for Lauren's reaction.

All went better than expected. My hard work on the house and Digger's cooperation received a reaction from Lauren that was priceless.

"Whose house is this?" she asked, thinking I was trying to trick her. "No really Jim, whose house did you bring me to?"

"Mine and Digger's," I said laughing and smiling from ear to ear.

"I was at your house after the funeral and I know for a fact it didn't look anything like this!" Lauren suddenly stopped and grew quiet before turning toward me and saying in a softer, caring voice, "Oh, I'm sorry, Jim. I wasn't thinking before I said that last comment. I hope I didn't upset you." And then she looked back at the house, "But really Jim, WOW! What a beautiful transformation. I love what you did with the wrap-around porch. It looks like a whole new house! Well done!"

"Well, thanks, missy. Your compliments mean a lot to Digger and me."

"Why Digger?" she asked.

Instead of answering her right away, I said, "Just wait. You'll soon see."

Lauren, Digger, and I went from room to room as I explained to Lauren in detail what was restored. She patiently listened as I talked about my dislike for wallpaper and my love of hardwood floors. I proudly pointed out the craftsmanship of each addition and when each of my ancestors contributed their work to the house.

"And last but not least, Digger's and my favorite improvement," I announced while opening the screened-in porch's door. The sun was setting in the perfect spot, and we all three froze in place taking in the beauty of the view for a moment.

"This is beautiful!" She sounded captured by the splendor of the sunset reflected in the lake below. I was busting at the seams with pride but didn't want to seem too obvious. I let Lauren soak it in for a little while longer before I asked her if she would like something to drink.

"Sure. What do you have?"

"I have beer, water, iced tea, or lemonade."

"Hmm, that sounds familiar. I would like iced tea, please, with lemon if you have it," she said.

"Coming right up. Be back soon." I entered the kitchen and threw the potatoes into the microwave, brought out the ice teas, and began to light the grill.

"Hope you like steak. It's about the only thing I know how to cook," I said apologetically.

"I sure do. Would you know how to cook a medium steak?" She asked.

"Yes, and dinner will be ready in a few minutes."

Lauren began looking at the backyard, and I could tell by the expression on her face she was confused by what she saw. Then she began to laugh.

"I get it now. This is Digger's work. Well, you sure earn your name," she said chuckling and rubbing his ears.

"So tell me again, what exactly was Digger's contribution?" she asked.

"After I filled in all of the holes in the front lawn and driveway, he didn't dig them up again," I said laughing. Lauren joined in the laughter while nodding her head in agreement.

I was hoping Lauren couldn't tell how nervous I was, counting on the evening to turn out just right. Fortunately, the steaks were cooked to perfection and everything else went as planned. I cleared the dinner dishes and walked into the kitchen to release a sigh of relief knowing dessert was going to be the easiest part.

Lauren insisted on helping me finish clearing the table and wash the dishes. I had installed a dishwasher when the kitchen was updated, but I didn't use it too often. I still preferred doing the dishes by hand. Keeping my hands busy would be calming and just what I needed for the disclosure, and this would allow me to say what was necessary to Lauren without looking at her. Lauren and I stood side by side at the sink. It was decided I would wash and she would put the dish into the dish-washer to dry. I took a deep breath and began.

"Lauren, there is something I must tell you. Please let me finish talking before you speak or I might not be able to go through with the whole story."

"Okay, Jim. It sounds serious. Apparently, it's weighing heavily on your mind. Is this the something else you had mentioned when we made this date?"

I nodded while keeping focused on the dishes.

"After I added the porches around the house and updated the inside, I packed up Judy's belongings and took them to church for the rummage sale."

Lauren couldn't help herself. "Oh, Jim, that must have been very hard emotionally for you," she said with a compassionate tone in her voice.

I nodded, unable to speak through the lump forming in my throat. After a few deep breaths, I pushed on.

"While I was at church Pastor Luke and I had a good conversation about our relationship."

A look of concern passed over Lauren's face and her interest grew, but she remained silent.

"I explained to Pastor Luke my concerns regarding the town talking about us. Most importantly any negative gossip directed towards you."

At this, Lauren couldn't contain herself any longer. "I'm a big girl, Jim, and as much as I am flattered by your concern for my reputation, I don't care what the 2&4 ladies are saying about us! But please continue. What did Pastor Luke have to say?"

"According to his viewpoint, there had been a proper mourning period since Judy's passing. He also spoke about how highly he thought of you, especially your generosity, talents, and integrity. He said that everyone who knows us is happy for us and we should enjoy what we have together. Lastly, he believed Judy would have wanted me to have someone special like you in my life. I agreed with him. Lauren, you are a beautiful and wonderful women and I love you."

It took all the courage I had to turn away from the sink and look into Lauren's eyes, relieved to see Lauren returning my gaze.

"I love you, too, Jim."

We followed our confession of love with deep, emotion-filled kisses. When we finally parted, we were both smiling from ear to ear.

Lauren took a deep breath and said, "I'm glad that we have the same feelings for one another. I was hoping you felt the same way about me as I did you."

"I had some things to work out. Working on the house helped me figure out most of it, and Pastor Luke helped me with the rest."

We finished up the dishes and spent the evening talking about the future together. I realized that, if this relationship was going to start off on the right foot, I had to come clean about everything to Lauren.

While driving Lauren back home I started, "If you're not busy, would you take a ride with Digger and me tomorrow on a road trip?"

"I don't have anything planned. Where are we going?"

"Well, Lauren, there's something else I must share with you, but this time I promise no blindfold. We'll pick you up at nine, and don't dress too nice, remember, Digger will be along. He may end up sharing more of the surrounding dirt and landscape than you would like." I hoped tomorrow's road trip wouldn't be our last.

Chapter 16

All morning there was a lump of lead in my stomach when I thought about the day ahead. I had hoped it would go as smoothly as the night before. I explained to Digger that we were going on a road trip and that he and I needed a shower. Digger loved water and it had always been an easy way to get him clean. Within the close quarters of the truck, the dirty-dog smell would have been an unpleasant experience for everyone but Digger.

When we both were clean, dry, and presentable, we loaded into the truck. Digger and I arrived at Lauren's house and spotted her sitting on the porch dressed in faded blue jeans and a pink tee-shirt. She looked cute as a button, and I told her so when I opened the door of the truck for her to get in. Digger greeted Lauren with a big hello of wet kisses and she laughed.

"Glad to see you too," she said rubbing his ears. She climbed into the truck. "Are you going to tell me where we're going yet?"

"I think it's best if you just wait until we get there. We are only going about an hour's ride south," I said.

We talked about many things along the way, and time seemed to fade until the exit signs began appearing on the highway. I felt the lump in my stomach join forces with the lump in my throat as we left the highway and maneuvered through town. Finally turning into the cemetery drive, I glanced at Lauren. "This is the cemetery where Judy is buried."

"Jim, why the big mystery? You could have told me earlier. Of course, I would go to the cemetery with you."

The cemetery was centuries old and deeds to plots were handed down through the families. Judy was a member of one of those families, and I knew being among her ancestors was where she would want to be buried.

I pulled the truck up and parked under the largest magnolia tree in the cemetery. Thankfully, Judy's family chose to be buried close to the magnolia, which provided plenty of shade for parking the car and a bench close by.

Digger began to whine with anticipation as he paced back and forth in the back seat. I looked to make sure there weren't any other visitors around and opened the back door. Digger shot out like a bullet and headed towards familiar ground.

"Digger, stop!" Lauren yelled and then looked back at me with concern.

"It's okay; he's been here before. Don't worry. He always comes back," I assured her.

We walked toward Judy's grave in silence. Lauren followed my lead, and I reached out for her hand for support. I knew this was an important closure for me. When we reached the gravesite, I started talking to Judy aloud, as if she was really there.

"Hello, sweetheart. I have brought someone with me today. She is a beautiful person both inside and out, and even though I know you're not really here, I wanted you two to meet."

Lauren's eyes welled up in tears and she added in a crackled voice, "Hello. I don't know exactly what to say, but I will speak from my heart. I love Jim as much as I could possibly love another human being. I can tell there are times when we're together that his mind drifts back to a time you two shared. This brings me not envy or frustration, but pure joy knowing his love runs deep, and I am privileged to be on the receiving end. I trust in his love which is matched by his compassion, integrity, and truth."

Expressing our feelings aloud resulted in teary eyes for both of us. We turned and held each other for a while until it dawned on me that I hadn't seen Digger lately.

"Digger!" I called.

On cue, Digger arrived with a piece of weathered wood about the size of a two-by-four, dragging it from one end. Proud of his treasure, he dropped the wood at my feet and waited for praise.

"What in the world?" Lauren exclaimed.

"This is the other reason I wanted you to take this trip with us today. You see, there is something else I want to share with you. Please try not to judge me or say anything until I finish the whole story."

Lauren nodded her head in agreement, and I picked up the wood Digger had dropped at my feet. I was grateful for something to occupy my attention while I recited the events and avoided eye contact with Lauren. We walked over to the bench and I began.

"When I first started coming here to visit Judy, it was just me, and the trip back was hard. Occasionally, I'd pull off on the side of the road until I could continue. I knew waiting for me back at Libertyville was an empty house full of memories of our life together. Fortunately, Digger was also waiting for me back home and he was my motivation. I began taking Digger everywhere including the trips to the cemetery.

"A while back, Digger and I made a trip to the cemetery, and I let him out of the truck since no one was around for him to annoy. Well, Digger did what Digger does and ventured off exploring. He came back with a similar piece of wood, just like he did today, prancing with his head held high. At first, I chuckled at how proud he looked with that old piece of wood hanging sideways out of his mouth. But then I picked up the wood for a better look, realizing it would be a good idea to investigate what Digger was up to. I feared Digger had been digging in the cemetery and we both could be in a heap of trouble. So I praised him and encouraged him to show me where he had gotten the wood. Satisfied with my praises, he was eager to show me where there was more wood to be found. With me hot on his trail, Digger trotted off in the same direction he came from. I let out a sigh of relief when he passed all of the tombs and headed into the woods.

"Deep in the woods, he was hard to keep up with, but eventually, he stopped at the edge of the Red River. Lying in a disorganized heap was a pile of weather-worn old wood, some half buried into the muddy bank and other pieces scattered around closer to the woods. I stood on the bank holding the wood Digger had brought me and felt pressed to gather the wood up and bring it back home. I wasn't thinking about why the wood was where Digger found it. I could tell it was good quality wood, and I had a plan to repurpose it into something useful and at the same time clean up the riverbank. I unloaded the wood from the bed of my truck the next morning. That is when things got a very strange."

I stopped and looked at Lauren. Her face reflected interest and I continued.

"There was this voice that occurred whenever I started touching the wood. It wasn't a voice I had ever heard before; and at first, I thought I was going off the deep end. Apparently, I was the only one that could hear the voice because Digger didn't seem to have a reaction when it started. At first, it was barely a whisper but then it grew louder and more demanding each day. The wood took on a life of its own and the voice provided instructions on how to recondition it and what the final piece would be when completed. The voice was feminine and specific down to the last detail. I was even instructed to deliver the piece to H&E before it opened on Saturday a few months back. The walnut wood was repurposed into a full-length mirror with adjustable wings on either side for a complete reflection.

"Do you remember the young couple with the baby that sat at our table at the church picnic?" I asked.

"Yes, Jac and Brian, right? I would see them around town. They are a cute couple."

"Right. Well, they went into H&E the same day, right after I had delivered the mirror, and bought it. Do you remember how super skinny Jac was for a while after they moved to Libertyville?"

"Yes, I was very concerned for her health. Just looking at her you could tell something was wrong," Lauren answered.

"She doesn't look that way now," I said.

"Jim, that was probably just a coincidence and the voice might have been your powerful creativity working overtime."

"Maybe, but hear me out, it gets more interesting.

"The mirror used up every last piece of usable walnut from Digger's find. So Digger and I made another trip to see Judy and check on the riverbank for any more old discarded wood. We walked upriver from where the first pile was located and found more wood. This wood was in much larger pieces and there was lots more of it.

After I paid my respects to Judy, I loaded the wood into the bed of the truck. There was so much of it and the wood was very heavy, so it took me till almost nightfall to get it loaded. The next day while unloading the wood the same thing happened again. The voice returned, only this time it was deeper and talked very slowly.

"The wood turned out to be hickory when reconditioned. The baseball bats, drumsticks, and easels were all made from that hickory wood. Each project was directed by the voice. I had learned from a previous bad experience to listen to the voice and follow what I heard without question. I doubted my sanity from the very beginning when this all started, but the voice never failed to surprise me with correct information.

"The bats I donated to the Stars are rumored— started by Ed—to be the main reason for the end of their losing streak. The drumsticks, you know firsthand, were what you thought was a contributing factor to the drum section of the band and its ability to keep a steady beat. The easels I don't think you know about.

"Alex, the gallery owner, worked the fireworks show with Pastor Luke and me. In conversation, I asked how the gallery was doing. Lauren, he shared with me that he had bought two easels from H&E Furniture and pictures that he sets on the easels sell within two weeks. Lauren, those easels were made from the same hickory wood and sold to H&E Furniture. I needed to confirm his claim for myself, so I went to the gallery to see if there was a rational explanation. Everything I just told you has got to be more than mere coincidence. Now, I don't know about you, but I am thinking there is more to this wood than meets the eye."

I grew silent and let Lauren digest everything I had said.

She looked at me and then to the piece of wood in my hand. She took longer to say anything than I would have liked. Finally, she spoke up.

"So everything that was said at the church picnic was really true?" she asked.

"I didn't think so at the time and I brushed it off as a coincidence, until I literally ran into Alex on my way to the fireworks stage."

She looked me straight in the eyes and said, "Jim, you have a theory of how the wood Digger found and you took home to repurpose was special. The wood not only spoke to you but also played an important part in Jac's life and her health, the Stars comeback, the band's improved performance, and the increased sales of art displayed at Gallery A. Before I can agree with your theory, I have a few questions for you."

"Go ahead ask me anything. I have nothing to hide from you."

"During the time you were working on the wood from the riverbank and the voice was coming to you, did you have an opportunity to make anything from any other wood?"

"Yes, I made other pieces out of wood from my shed and also wood I bought from Ray. And no, Lauren, to answer your next question, I didn't hear any voices. I have never in my life experienced anything like it," I said, shaking my head from side to side.

"Okay. Did you happen to stop and think about where you were when Digger found the wood?" she asked. "I mean, you were in a cemetery."

"Not really. I didn't give it much thought. The floods wash all sorts of materials onto the riverbank.

"Jim, you could have been using wood from some-one's casket! Did you even consider that as a possibility?" Lauren had a serious look on her face.

I stared down at the ground and answered her question.

"Yes, actually, that did cross my mind, but since it was all broken up and in pieces, it was pretty much unrecognizable and, truthfully, I didn't want to know."

"Do you want to know now?" Lauren asked.

"Yes, I do. The wood with the voice has not only influenced our lives but the lives of others. We need to find out more information."

"I am interested in why you didn't return to get more wood when the second load was used up?" Lauren asked.

"I was more interested in you, the house, and the Fourth's events at church. I didn't feel the need to return as often, and I was pretty busy. But I can tell you this: The wood can't be from a barn. No one would use walnut or hickory wood to build a barn. We could start looking for tombs missing caskets if you're interested in helping me solve this mystery," I said.

"I know whom to ask for more help in figuring this out! I will ask Douglas for his help. He is the history teacher at school and a bit of a Red River Parish historian," Lauren said.

I was impressed by Lauren's reaction to the full disclosure of the wood and the events surrounding it. I didn't know exactly what to expect from Lauren when

I told her about the voice and the wood, so I was totally relieved when she listened to all of the information and then came up with a plan to fill in the missing pieces. Mostly, I appreciated the fact she didn't think I was crazy.

"Would you have to tell Douglas the whole story?" I didn't want it known around town that I heard voices, nor the possibility I was using wood from people's caskets for various projects.

Lauren quickly understood my concerns. "I'll explain how Digger found the wood, and you and I are interested in knowing its origin, if possible."

"I really like that idea, no mention of voices and no lies either," I said.

The truck ride back to town was a little too quiet, and I was concerned Lauren maybe was having second thoughts about us. I knew I had just given her a lot of information to digest and she needed time and space to sort things out. When we arrived back at her house, Lauren kissed me and said she would call soon with any information. I told her I loved her and thanked her for being with me and believing in me. She smiled and then turned toward the house leaving me questioning my decision to open up about the wood.

Chapter 17

The next day, Lauren contacted Douglas, and he was excited to do the research. Lauren offered to help him, and she became so busy with the investigation that we were unable to see each other for a couple of weeks. Every evening Lauren would call and bring me up to date on the progress they were making. Douglas had access to records and documents that proved to be a big help in narrowing down information. They were getting close to tracing the wood's origin.

I was beginning to feel envious of Douglas being able to spend so much time with Lauren. I missed her face, her laugh, and the feel of her hand in mine.

Two weeks later, I could hear the excitement in Lauren's voice when I answered the phone. They were finished with the research. Douglas and Lauren wanted to share their findings and asked if I would be available for dinner at six this Saturday.

"Wild horses wouldn't keep me away!" I said, excited to be able to see Lauren again and also get to the bottom of the wood mystery.

I started getting ready at three and told Digger I was going out and wouldn't be back for a while. I checked and rechecked his water dish and the doggie door before leaving. I made it into town just in time to buy a box of chocolate covered cherries from the 5&10 and a bouquet of pink roses from Magnolia's before the stores closed. My plan was to arrive on the early side so Lauren and I could have some alone time.

I rang the doorbell and waited with the flowers and candy hidden behind my back. I love to see the look of surprise on Lauren's face and was hoping the gifts would do the trick. Lauren opened the door wide.

"Hello, handsome. I sure missed you." Lauren's face was lit up displaying a beautiful smile and her eyes danced with excitement.

I stepped through the doorway and presented the candy and flowers. "Sweets for the sweet and roses which next to your beauty appear pale. I practiced that all day," I said and then thought how truly corny it sounded and I felt somewhat embarrassed.

I was then rewarded with that look of surprise from Lauren I was hoping for.

"My, my. Thank you." She reached for my face and kissed me, erasing all doubt.

"Follow me back to the kitchen while I finish up dinner. We can put those roses in some water and set them on the table for a centerpiece."

Lauren retrieved a large crystal vase from the dining room curio and continued walking toward the kitchen. She then carefully placed the vase in my hands.

"Here you are, and thank you again for the lovely flowers," while planting a brief but sweet kiss on my lips.

"I hope it's okay that I'm a bit early, but I didn't exactly want an audience for our first contact in weeks," I said while filling the vase with water.

"I'm glad you did. Douglas and I have been so knee-deep in the research, you and I haven't been able to get together at all."

"Whew," I sighed with relief.

"What's that all about?" she asked.

"I thought after our trip together it had set you off and you didn't want to be around me anymore."

"Oh, that's my fault. I'm so sorry. I have a tendency to get so engrossed in things I become a hermit. I actually enjoyed the hunt for the information. Please forgive me."

"Sure, but it will cost you a kiss."

"Well, what are you waiting for?" And with that I pulled her close and kissed her until we were both breathless.

Unfortunately, the doorbell rang and we were forced to part.

"That must be Douglas," she said walking to the door.

I followed her, anxious to meet Douglas and check out the guy she had been spending so much time with the past two weeks. When Lauren opened the door and introduced us, I was surprised to find Douglas was a slight-build, older gentleman with specs and a graying beard. I was careful not to squeeze too hard when we shook hands. I had imagined him to be a much bigger, younger, and more handsome fellow who was after my gal. I laughed to myself at how foolish I had been.

"Come on in and make yourself at home. Dinner is going on the table," Lauren said as she walked back to the kitchen.

"Is there anything I can do to help?"

"Yes, why don't you find out what Douglas would like to drink? You know the list by now. I'll take an iced tea with lemon, please."

After getting the drinks, I helped Lauren get the rest of the meal onto the table. She had outdone herself with homemade lasagna, garlic bread, and a garden salad. Everything was delicious but I refused the third helping of lasagna that Lauren offered, knowing she had cheesecake for dessert. After coffee and dessert, we cleared the table and made room for the contents of Douglas' briefcase. He pulled out a laptop and copies of official documents and spread them on the table. After everything was in its proper place, he began.

"Lauren has been a big help in putting this together. She is much better with computers than I am," he said with a wink at Lauren.

"There is a whole lot of information gathered here, but to put it plain and simple, the flood two years ago was so intense it flooded cemeteries up and down the Red River. I'm sure you're aware of the ongoing issue of flooding in the cemeteries. Here in Louisiana we place the caskets in raised tombs or vaults. They are not buried. Flood waters will pop the cement tombs and vaults right out of the ground and then destroy the contents. Just like it destroys everything else in its path.

"Many caskets, remains, and tombs were misplaced by the flood waters from the Red River. Most of the caskets and tombs were recovered and reset but some were not so lucky, though, and the whereabouts of those caskets are still a mystery. I believe the wood you and Digger discovered is from those missing caskets. Lauren and I were able to dig—No pun intended—a little deeper and found information about the missing casket occupants, their families, and the cemeteries. She compiled a list on the computer and included comments from the obituaries and the death certificates," he said as he turned the computer toward me.

I began reading Lauren's list. It was broken down according to cemeteries, names, dates, cause of death, and then additional information on each in the comments.

"If I were to guess where the wood you found came from, I would start with the closest cemetery upstream of the wood's location. Then if you could find out the type of wood and approximate size of the coffin you would be able to narrow it down. But that would still only be a guess, since you wouldn't really know for sure."

"Do you have a printout of this information?" I asked.

"Yes, I thought you might ask for one. Here it is."

"I have a copy in my computer, too," Lauren added.

Since we knew where the wood was found, Lauren and I we were able to follow the map back up the Red River to the first cemetery on Douglas' list. There were six missing caskets in that particular cemetery and, apparently, the families were not interested in pursuing their recovery.

After a while, Douglas began gathering the papers and his laptop from the table and returned them to his briefcase.

"I believe you have enough information to solve the mystery of the wood's origin. So I'll leave you two to put the rest of the pieces of the puzzle together. If you need anything else, don't hesitate to ask. This was all very informative, Lauren. I enjoyed working with you on the project."

"Douglas, do I owe you anything for your time and trouble?" I asked.

"No, sir. I enjoyed researching something different for a change. These days everyone wants to know about their ancestors, ever since it became popular on those Internet sites."

"How about a little lasagna to go," Lauren offered.

"Now that, I'll take. I'm single and home cooking is a rare treat," Douglas replied.

Lauren packed up a container of lasagna, with some garlic bread and a slice of cheesecake. I walked with Douglas to the door and Lauren appeared with his doggie bag.

"I can't thank you enough. I'll let you know if we match the wood to any of the caskets on the list," she said.

"I hope it will be helpful. Thank you, Lauren. Everything was delicious. Good night, ya'll," he said as he accepted the doggie bag and disappeared down the steps into the night.

Lauren and I could hardly wait for Douglas to leave before we returned to reviewing the list. She had already narrowed the most likely of the six possibilities down to three. She turned the pages to where all three were marked, then asked me to read each one and see if there were any possibilities of a match.

"This one sounds like it was the first load of wood," I said and read the information to Lauren. "A young woman from apparently a wealthy family passed from anorexia according to the death certificate. That would match the female voice I heard and the high-quality wood used for her casket."

"Wasn't that the walnut wood you made the mirror from?" Lauren asked.

"Yes, it was." I went back to reading the entries. "Okay, one down. Let's see if we can find a match for the hickory wood."

"This older man who died of natural causes doesn't fit the size and bulk of the hickory wood, but this one does." I turned the page to read more of the comments. "He was almost seven feet tall and weighed well over 400 pounds. He was apparently the brunt of jokes and pranks because of his enormous size and strength. People called him 'Ox' because his dad often made him pull the plow. The cause of death is listed as a coronary. I'd wager a bet he was pulling a plow when it happened. That fits the profile exactly. They would have had to make a casket out of the strongest wood available and three times the size."

We both turned to each other and smiled with the realization we had just discovered the source of the wood, the reasons behind what the caskets were made into and why.

"The young woman's casket of walnut wood was instrumental in changing Jac's opinion of herself and restoring her health. As if the young woman's spirit was determined to correct a wrong from the past."

The hickory wood from Ox's casket helped the Stars, the band, and the artists at Gallery A to gain confidence and succeed when there was once doubt," Lauren said sharing our thoughts aloud. I nodded in agreement.

"Now what do we do?" I asked looking into Lauren's eyes. "We both know there is a lot more wood out there."

"And a lot more people to help," she said returning my gaze with sincerity.

"If you and Digger are up for the adventure, this little lady is too."

"I wouldn't want anyone else by my side," and I leaned in for a long-awaited kiss.

Acknowledgement

Repurposed Life is a true work from the heart, an idea planted while making funeral arrangements for my mother.

This book would not have been written if not for the continued support and encouragement of some very special people.

First and foremost, a huge thank you for tolerating the odd hours of writing, the closed doors, and everything else endured during this process. Fred Morris, I love you and appreciate you always allowing me to be me. I thank God for you every day!

Also, thank you to my family, friends, neighbors, and editor who kindly donated either their time, talent or encouragement, especially Lorraine and Joel Amant, Alia, Leslie and Theo Khoury, Lynn Lammlein, Pat Peterson and Kay Uhles.

The first names of the characters were used as a tribute to those loved ones that have passed from this earthly plane. Hil, Ethel, Fred, Gloria, Jim, Brian, Jacquelyn, Judy, Lauren, Luke, Ray, Marg, Douglas, Ruby, Ed, Pat, and Alex, a lifelong neighbor.

About the Author

Lyn Morris is the owner of Heartalk, LLC. She holds the title of Reiki Master and practices various other healing energy methods to help animals and humans alike.

She has learned to listen to spirit for guidance when applying energy work. With pure heart energy to assist in healing and providing insight, she asks and listens to Spirit for the best possible outcome for each client.

Repurposed Life was conceived while making her mother's funeral arrangements. After retiring from thirty years in the mortgage business, her first novel became a reality and was completed exactly three years to the date of her mother's passing.

She often was awakened at odd hours of the night and received inspirational information from Spirit while writing the novel. Till this day she is amazed by the assistance one receives from Spirit when open to the possibility of an answer. And that answer can arrive in many forms and fashions.

There is always a plan.

Sometimes you're the pebble tossed in the pond and sometimes you're the ripple.

www.ingramcontent.com/pod-product-compliance
Lightning Source LLC
Chambersburg PA
CBHW071528100726
47908CB00004B/1326